# Past Praise for
# the Witches of Orkney series

### Praise for *The Blue Witch:*

2019 American Fiction Awards:
Best Cover Design: Children's Books—Finalist

2019 American Fiction Awards:
Juvenile Fiction—Winner

2019 Readers' Favorite Awards
Gold Medal Winner in Children's Mythology/Fairy Tale

2019 Moonbeam: Gold Medal Winner
in Pre-Teen Fiction/Fantasy

"An enchanting new book full of magical mischief and adventure, Alane Adams's *The Blue Witch* is guaranteed to please."
—*Foreword Clarion Reviews*

"Bright, brave characters star in this exhilarating tale of magic and mystical creatures."
—*Kirkus Reviews*

## Praise for *The Rubicus Prophecy:*

"Adams' concise prose delivers a quick read that's packed with colorful characters and subplots . . . Returning illustrator Stroh's bold black-and-white artwork, as in the previous book, perfectly captures the author's stunningly detailed world."

—*Kirkus Reviews*

# Witch Wars

Published by SparkPress, a BookSparks imprint,
A division of SparkPoint Studio, LLC
Phoenix, Arizona, USA, 85007
www.gosparkpress.com

Published 2020
Printed in the United States of America
ISBN: 978-1-68463-063-9 (pbk)
ISBN: 978-1-68463-064-6 (e-bk)

Library of Congress Control Number: 2020907168

Illustrations by Jonathan Stroh
Interior design by Tabitha Lahr

Witches of Orkney
Volume Three:

ALANE ADAMS

To My Sutton Rae

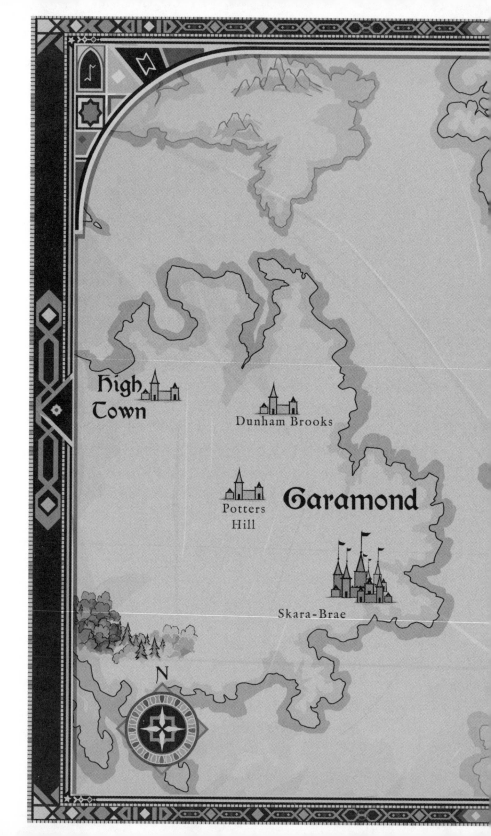

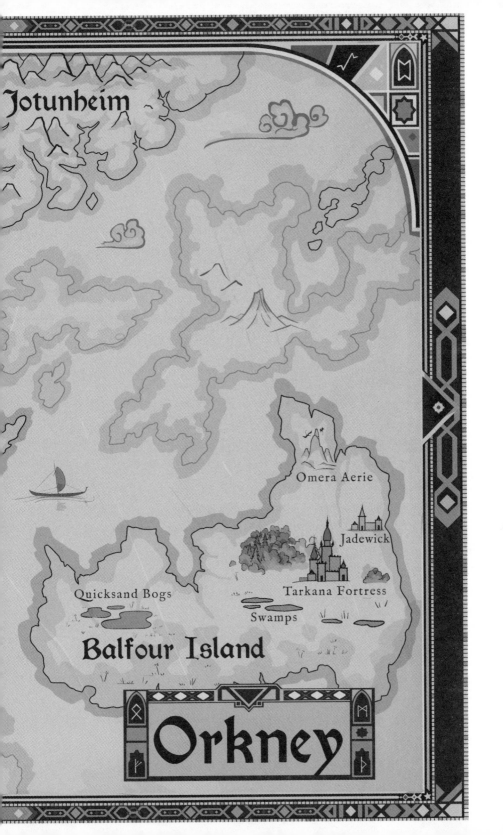

# Prologue

## Asgard

## Ancient Days

I duna gathered her apples, carefully plucking them from the sacred tree. As the goddess of youth and caretaker of the apples that gave the gods their immortality, she was tasked with harvesting the fruit daily and carrying a basketful to the hall of the gods to hand out.

As she made her way to the grand hall where the gods waited, a familiar youth fell into step beside her. For days now, everywhere Iduna went, the same charming young man had appeared out of nowhere, retrieving her handkerchief when she dropped it, gripping her elbow when she was jostled in the marketplace, and offering to carry her basket of apples. It might have bothered her if he wasn't so charming.

"We meet again," he said with his cheeky grin.

"Indeed," she answered. "What brings you to the city of the gods?"

"I'm hoping to apprentice to the god of archery. Ull is training me to shoot an arrow through the eye of a gnat."

Iduna smiled at the thought. The lad seemed too slight to wield a bow. She should shoo him away, but honestly, she rather enjoyed his company. It wasn't often anyone spoke to her, and it got lonely tending to her tree all alone.

"Humans aren't usually allowed in Asgard," she replied. "How did you come to be invited?"

"My father is famous for making the best bows in all of Midgard," he boasted. "He sent me to bring one to Ull as a gift in return for my training."

Iduna's foot hit a rock, and she tumbled, spilling her basket of precious apples across the paving stones.

"Here, let me help." The young man hurried to gather them up in his shirttail, then returned to dump them in her basket.

"Thank you," she said, nursing her stinging palms. "I don't know how I tripped." She looked around, but there was no sign of a stone out of place. "I guess I'm clumsy today. What did you say your name was?"

The young man sketched a short bow. "Vertulious, at your service." He held one of her sacred apples in his hands, frowning as he polished it on his shirt. "I'm afraid this one is bruised, surely unfit for a god. You don't mind if I keep it, do you?"

All good humor left her. "Those belong to the gods." She held her hand out, suddenly wary of the sly look in his eyes.

He dropped the apple onto her palm. "Well, then you should keep a close eye on them. You wouldn't want one to go missing." He tapped his fingers to his forehead and spun around, cheerily whistling as he marched off.

Iduna watched him go, a slight shiver running up her spine. She carefully counted the apples in her basket, relieved when she accounted for them all.

Vertulious could barely contain his excitement. After so many years of searching, he had found the sacred garden and the goddess who oversaw it. His hand went to the round globe in his cloak pocket. She hadn't seen him tuck it away as he'd gathered the spilled fruit, replacing the one he'd taken with an ordinary apple. One god would not gain the customary life-restoring powers the apples offered—instead he or she would experience mild discomfort, perhaps a headache or an ache in their bones, and then would partake of another magical apple tomorrow and forget all about it.

While he would harvest everything there was to know about this apple. Every element. Every ingredient. Until he unlocked its secrets.

Eager to get back to his laboratory, Vertulious was making his way to the Bifrost bridge, the passageway back to Midgard, when a sharp voice called out.

"Say, boy, what are you doing in the city of the gods?"

Vertulious held still, reminding himself he was but a hapless youth. "Nothing, your godness." He turned, and his tongue grew thick as he took in the forbidding figure of Thor, god of thunder and Son of Odin. He was standing in his carriage pulled by his two brawny goats, their wicked horns as thick as a man's arm and curving back to sharp points. His famed hammer, Mjolnir, was strapped to his side. Around his waist he wore his Belt of Strength, and his famed gauntlets—large golden gloves—encased his hands.

"I've seen you hanging around here for a few days," the god said, "but no one seems to know who you are or why you are here."

Vertulious bowed low. "It is an honor to be in your presence. I was sent by my father to bring a gift to Ull in hopes he would apprentice me, but he found my talents lacking, so I am going home."

Thor's frown relaxed a tad. "Ull is known to be difficult. I am sorry you wasted a journey."

Vertulious kicked at a loose pebble. "It's okay. I have been a disappointment to my father since I was born. This will not change anything." He backed away, hoping Thor would leave it be, but the annoying god had a soft heart.

"Perhaps you could apprentice with me. My servant Thialfi has gone home to tend to his herd. I am in need of someone to polish my hammer until he returns." He tapped the heavy weapon.

Vertulious eyed it greedily, wondering if it would be worth stealing, but he let the idea go. Possessing the power of Thor's hammer would not get him what he desired, but Thor would expect him to agree.

"It would be an honor," he said with a bow. "I can think of no one more powerful than the mighty god Thor. I will go home and tell my father and arrange to return."

"Come. You may ride with me. I have business in the land of men. It is a long journey down the Bifrost bridge for a human."

Vertulious bowed again and sat on the back of the chariot, dangling his legs as the god raced down the rainbow bridge back to Midgard, grateful Thor couldn't see the grin that split his face.

After promising to meet again in three days' time, Vertulious hurried away into the woods, letting himself age back to his normal self. With the transformation came the aches and pains that riddled his old body. By the time he reached his lab, night had fallen, and his bones were weary, but he lit an oil lamp, too excited to sleep.

Plucking the apple from his pocket, he placed it on the table. He waved a hand over it, and it lifted, spinning slowly. He inhaled deeply, savoring the magic that oozed from the red globe.

Finally, the formula to eternal life was in his grasp— the greatest spell an alchemist could perform. All he had to do was unlock the secrets of this simple fruit. First things first, he would have to isolate each element that made up the apple's potent magic.

He dared cut the precious fruit open and took a bite. Energy zinged through him, fueling him with vigor as he worked through the night, taking careful notes. In the skin, he found traces of sulfire and radion. In the stem, hints of lizardine. He removed the seeds and ground them down to a paste, pleased to find vanadium and oullium. All plentiful elements—but one element eluded him. A faint green sparkle in the flesh of the apple itself.

Then he remembered a small green stone he had found one day in his travels. He rummaged through his shelves, tossing containers aside until he found the faintly glowing bottle. He blew away the layer of dust.

Turnium. So rare he had only ever found this small pebble.

Pleased, he placed the ingredients in a cauldron and began reciting the transformation spell, but no amount of magic would change them into the sacred fruit. He needed a source of power—one so great it came from the gods themselves. But what?

His thoughts were interrupted by a knocking on his door. He opened it to find dawn had broken. Rubicus stood there, one hand to his jaw.

"Where have you been hiding yourself, Verty?" the he-witch blustered, pushing his way in. "My tooth has been aching for days, but you've ignored my messages."

"You know how it is. An alchemist's work is never finished."

"What are you working on?" Rubicus eyed the scattered ingredients curiously.

"A cure for the pox," Vertulious drawled, earning a roll of the eyes from the he-witch. "Really, I'm quite busy."

"This can't wait. You'll never guess who is roaming the woods—the high and mighty Thor and two Valkyrie warriors. They're looking for a boy who dared steal something from them."

Vertulious's blood went cold. "Are they now?"

"Yes. Please, Verty. My tooth is killing me."

Vertulious thought desperately. He couldn't lose his work, not when he was so close. It could take him years to find a source of power to complete the spell—maybe decades. He needed time—time he didn't have. His mortal body was failing him even as his mind remained sharp.

If only there was a way to preserve his mind until he had the necessary tools . . . and then a thought came to him. *Yes.* That is what he would do. "I can fix your tooth. I have just the thing."

Rubicus took a seat, and Vertulious rolled the small stone between his thumb and finger as he muttered a spell to soften it. Reaching back into Rubicus's mouth, he shoved the turnium into the rotted tooth, sealing it in place.

"Better?"

Rubicus worked his jaw. "Amazing. You're a genius, Verty."

As soon as the he-witch was gone, Vertulious threw some things into a bag. There was still a chance he could flee before the god of thunder descended. At least for now, the turnium was safe.

He was just reaching for his spellbook when a pounding sounded on his door. Before he could answer, the door blew open, splintering off its hinges. Thor stood in the entry, his hammer clenched in his fist.

"You stole one of my father's apples."

Vertulious wanted to lie, but the remains of the apple were scattered over the table. Behind Thor, the fair Iduna eyed him accusingly, along with a pair of fierce-looking Valkyrie warriors in their golden regalia, gripping swords.

"It was one apple. Surely the gods can spare a bit of immortality in the name of science," he quipped, shrugging his shoulders.

Thor spun the hammer in his hand, the metal head a blur. "You have underestimated my father. He does not like to share. Not one apple. Ever. Prepare to die." He raised the hammer and threw it, sending it spinning straight for Vertulious.

Only the hammer went right through him. Vertulious vanished, changing into a wisp of energy that floated in the air above Thor's head, and then zinged into the open spellbook on the table.

# Chapter 1

Large flakes of snow drifted lazily from an iron sky, covering the Tarkana swamps in a winter blanket. Abigail ignored the cold, her hands stuffed into the pockets of her cloak as she marched along. This was all her fault, she reminded herself for the millionth time. All of it. The return of that horrible he-witch Vertulious. The demise of Endera's mother. The threat of war hanging over everyone's head. If only she had never picked up that stupid spellbook.

She doubled her pace, clutching her book bag over her shoulder. The worst part had been facing Endera. The witchling had been ordered to return to class after days locked away in her room, but the pain on her face was etched deep. She wouldn't even look at Abigail—staring past her as if she were invisible.

It didn't matter that Hugo insisted Abigail shouldn't blame herself. Hugo was wrong.

Abigail paused, watching her breath fog in the wintry air. The swamps were eerily quiet. Gassy burps erupted out of the ground, shifting clumps of snow. Shreeks nested in the trees, eyeing her with red eyes but not daring to spread their wings lest they freeze.

Two months had passed since the night Vertulious returned, and so much had changed it made Abigail's head spin.

*War.*

That was all anyone ever talked about, and Abigail was sick of it. Already, details of older witchlings had been sent off on secret missions. There had been no actual battles yet, just rumors that grew wilder and wilder, but it was only a matter of time.

She continued on until she broke through the trees and stood on the edge of a bluff overlooking the sea. Waves crashed against the rocks below. Reaching into her bag, she pulled out the leather-bound book that had caused so much trouble. The spellbook was empty now, the pages blank. Abigail hefted it in her hands, waiting to see if she felt anything, but it no longer had the power to call to her.

It didn't make her hate it any less.

She raised it over her head and threw it over the edge, watching it spin through the air. It hit the water with a satisfying splash and then sank from sight. Relief washed over her. She stared out at the horizon, wishing she could see the sails of a familiar Orkadian warship.

Robert was long gone. Never to return to their island. Never to face the friends who had betrayed him.

"I miss him too."

She didn't turn, unsurprised Hugo had followed her. "Do you think he's still angry at us?"

"He has every reason to be."

They were talking about Robert Barconian, of course—the one-time friend they had abandoned when he'd called on them to stand for him. Abigail had wanted to take his side that horrible night Vertulious had returned, but Madame Vex had silenced her, reminding her of her duty to the coven.

"If Emenor hadn't practically throttled me, I would have spoken up, you know," Hugo said.

"Me too." She sighed. "Do you suppose we'll ever see him again?"

"On the other side of a battlefield perhaps."

Her chest tightened at the thought. She turned to face Hugo. He wore the black uniform of the Balfin Boys' Brigade, even though she knew he hated it. Fresh bruises marked his face. The other boys still picked on him for preferring science over brigade training, but he didn't complain. "Why did you follow me?"

"I've been thinking. About the vision Calla's mother had."

Calla's mother was a witch named Calista who preferred to take the form of a mermaid. "About how if we go to war, the gods will erase this place as if it never existed?"

"Yes. Do you think it's true?"

"Odin brought these islands here. He can just as easily get rid of them."

"But what about the people?" Hugo protested. "Doesn't he care about them?"

She shrugged. "Probably. I don't know."

Hugo sighed. "I wish things could go back to the way they were."

"That's never going to happen as long as Vertulious is here," she said bitterly. "He's determined to rule Orkney. He has the entire coven hanging on his every word."

"Like Safina used to hang on yours."

Pain needled Abigail. Safina, once her sweet protégé, now refused to speak to her—becoming Endera's pet instead.

She turned to stare back out at the cold sea. "Safina's misled. Like the rest of the coven, she's put her faith in the wrong person. Endera doesn't care about her any more than Vertulious cares about us. He'll destroy anything that stands in his way."

"So what are we going to do about it?"

"We?" She looked sideways at him. "What can *we* do? Vertulious is too powerful by far."

"So we stand by and let him start a war that will destroy this place and everyone in it?"

Abigail planted her hands on her hips. "What would you have us do, Hugo? I'm a witch. When it mattered most, I turned my back on a friend to be loyal to my coven."

"Proving what?"

"That my heart is made of stone."

He stared at her as though she'd grown an extra head. "I know this has been hard, Abigail. Losing your mother all over again. Seeing Melistra destroyed and having Endera blame you."

"She's right to blame me—if I'd never been born, none of this would have happened." Her hand strayed to her pocket, searching for the soothing object she carried.

"Maybe . . . but the fact is you were born. Your father was a beautiful star. And your mother loved you so much she came back to save you." Hugo drew her hand out and uncurled her fingers. A small white stone nestled in her palm: a single teardrop from her mother. "This stone represents her love for you," he said quietly.

Abigail blinked back tears, fighting the pain that came with thinking about her mother. "How do you know that? Maybe it means nothing. Maybe it's just a dumb crystal."

"Then toss it into the sea."

Annoyed, she jerked her hand free and dropped the stone back into her pocket. "I have to go. I don't want to be late for classes." She brushed past him and headed back along the trail of footprints in the snow.

"I'm going to find a way to stop this," he called. "With or without your help."

Abigail paused at the edge of the woods, then turned to give him a cool stare. "You're a Balfin. You serve the witches. Or have you forgotten?"

"I serve what's right. And war is never right. You know that."

"War is war, Hugo. Why are you such a child? Maybe we should stop meeting all the time until you grow up."

Hurt flickered across his face. "I thought you were my friend."

"So did Robert," she snapped.

Hugo flinched, as she had intended. "Yeah, well, he thought the same about you."

# Chapter 2

Abigail hurried to her first class, already regretting her words to Hugo. She would have to apologize later. For now she had to get through Awful Alchemy. It used to be her favorite class. In fact, she had been Madame Malaria's star pupil, but no longer. Not since the day Vertulious had returned. One of the first things he had done was remove Madame Malaria from her position and take over teaching her classes.

Abigail took her seat in the back row, as far away from the front as possible. The other witchlings were all seated, eagerly waiting for the revered he-witch to appear.

Calla dropped into the seat next to her. "Is it gone?" she asked quietly.

Abigail nodded as the side door that led to the alchemist's private chambers opened. Vertulious stepped into the classroom carrying a small draped cage, which he set on a table. Shimmering threads laced his blue robes, and he'd tucked his silvery hair under a matching blue skullcap. He searched the room, not stopping until his eyes met Abigail's, and a satisfied smile curved his lips.

"Secondlings. We have learned much in the weeks we have been together. Today we will see who can impress me with her newfound powers. The witchling who can complete this spell will be my personal assistant for the rest of the term."

An excited rustle of whispers broke out. It would be a huge honor for any of them to be recognized. Abigail was probably the only one who dreaded it.

Vertulious pulled the drape off the cage, revealing a small shreek. It hissed at the alchemist, spraying green spittle. "To earn my favor, you must use the metamorphis spell we learned earlier this week to turn this lowly shreek into an Omera."

The classroom gasped and groaned at the same time. Turning a spotted moth into a butterfly, maybe, but changing such a low-level creature into a fierce and powerful Omera was far beyond their reach. Abigail snorted, thinking it ridiculous.

"What is that, Abigail?" Vertulious asked. "Do you not think your fellow classmates are up to such a challenge?"

His eyes were like lightning rods, pinning her in place.

She straightened, clearing her throat. "If they can, they deserve to be Head Witchling."

Vertulious beckoned her forward. "Come here and I'll assist you."

Endera shot up, planting her hands on her desk. "That's not fair if you help Abigail."

Vertulious eyed her coolly. "Would you like to volunteer then? Your mother certainly didn't mind."

The girl went pale as milk, but her eyes glittered at the alchemist. "Better me than Abigail." She stepped around the desk and moved to the front of the class.

Abigail rested her chin on her hands, curious to see what Vertulious was up to.

"What have we learned is the secret to performing alchemy spells?" he asked.

"That you need the proper catalyst and a source of power," Endera replied, repeating the words he had drilled into their heads.

"Correct. I was able to return to my original form thanks to a collection of elements I assembled and Abigail's assistance unlocking the power in Odin's Stone."

Endera went even paler—that spell had destroyed her mother in the process, but Vertulious ignored her distress as he went on.

"The metamorphis spell can change the form of one being into a completely new one, if you possess the right keys. Tell me, what are the keys to transform this hapless shreek into a powerful and vicious Omera?"

Endera's brow furrowed, but finally she shrugged. "I don't know."

"Then you may sit down." He turned his back on her. "Who can tell me what is needed to complete the spell?"

Endera stood frozen. For a moment, Abigail thought she might plant a ball of witchfire in the old alchemist's backside, but she spun on her heel and returned to her desk, taking her seat and staring down at the floor.

Portia raised her hand. The girl had taken a liking to Vertulious after Madame Malaria had given her a pox on her face earlier in the term.

Vertulious nodded at her.

She stood, smoothing her skirt with her hands. "I think the shreek needs something that will make it grow, since the Omera is much larger."

Vertulious nodded. "Go on."

Portia glowed. "We learned in Horrid Hexes how to make someone's feet grow by putting a pinch of gallillium in their porridge. What if we fed some to the shreek and used the metamorphis spell?"

"It's a start. But not enough. Sit down."

Portia gaped, then thought better of saying anything, slumping down in her seat.

"A child could make this shreek bigger," Vertulious scolded. "That won't make it an Omera. What do we know of these blackhearted creatures?"

The Omera were known to be fierce, although Abigail had met Big Mama and her offspring, and they were different. She smiled fondly thinking about them.

"Abigail, I hear you have met an Omera before. Even tamed one. Come, share with the class." He beckoned her forward.

Abigail stood, knowing if she didn't, he would simply force her feet to move. On her way to the front, she passed Endera, who trembled with rage.

"Tell the class what you know about these magnificent creatures." Vertulious had a calculating look in his eyes. He was up to something, but she couldn't decipher what it was.

"They're not all bad," she ventured. "I met some that were kind of nice."

Vertulious laughed. "Nice? An Omera can rip a man to shreds with just its talons. Did you know the Omera were created centuries ago by a Volgrim witch to fight at our side? It has been eons since this coven had the power to control them. It is time we showed them who they work for."

"They're wild animals, not pets," Abigail said. "We can't control them or own them." The very thought was appalling.

"The Omera have forgotten who they belong to," Vertulious replied icily. "We created them. We rule over them. We just need to remind them of that and bring them to heel."

Abigail stared at the cruelty in his eyes, thinking of Big Mama and her little babes. They weren't meant to be tamed, but before she could argue, he clamped a hand on her shoulder.

"Come, let's do the metamorphis spell together, shall we?"

A sudden suspicion made the hair on the back of her neck rise. He was pulling strings like a puppeteer, getting her in front of the class like this—but why? Then the answer was obvious. *He must not be able to do it by himself, or he would have done so.* Abigail shrugged free and took a step back. "No. I'm not going to help you."

His eyes hardened into steel points. "This class is an important part of your placement here at the Tarkana Witch Academy. I would hate for you to be expelled."

Abigail gasped. He would never . . . but she read the coldness in his stare. He didn't really care. Right now, he needed her to help him with this metamorphis spell, and nothing else mattered.

Vertulious unscrewed the lid on a jar. Abigail recognized the ingredient, gallillium, the same one Portia had mentioned.

He opened the cage door—ignoring the spitting, hissing shreek—and snapped his fingers. The shreek froze on its perch. He pried open its beak, sprinkling some of the gallillium powder down its throat.

"Now, class, the gallillium will make the shreek bigger, but to create metamorphis, we need something from an Omera to spark the change." He reached into his robes and pulled out a pointed tooth. "Like this fang I found walking in the swamps one day." He waved his left hand, causing the air in front of the shreek to swirl. The creature's eyes moved wildly from side to side as a hole in its chest grew larger.

*Was that its tiny heart beating away?*

Vertulious slipped the fang into its chest and then waggled his finger.

The hole sealed up, and the shreek shook itself, hissing at them.

"Now say the words with me," Vertulious said. "*Cabela ello morpheus.*"

Abigail remained mute. This was wrong. If she was expelled, so be it.

The alchemist leaned in and spoke in her ear. "Do it now, or your little Balfin friend might have a terrible accident."

Abigail's heart clenched.

"Don't be shy," Vertulious said loudly. "Everyone is waiting."

The whole class had gone silent. Even Endera raised her eyes to see what would happen next.

Abigail took a deep breath, hating herself but knowing she didn't have a choice. "*Cabela ello morpheus.*"

"Now a source of power." Vertulious raised his hand and unleashed a blaze of green witchfire that circled the cage and made the shreek freeze. "Join me," he commanded.

Reluctantly, she raised her hands and released her own blast of witchfire. Oddly, he didn't ask her to remove her sea emerald, so her witchfire was as green as his.

The class oohed as their twin blasts of witchfire joined, turning the cage into a glowing orb that lifted off the table, then simply disappeared. The shreek remained trapped in the center of the ball of light.

"Repeat the words again," he said.

Abigail wanted to resist, but Hugo's face flashed in front of her.

"*Cabela ello morpheus.*"

The shreek began to spin in the air, twirling faster and faster until it was a blur. A ball of mist grew larger and larger around it, shrouding it from sight.

Finally, Vertulious held a hand up, and Abigail dropped her hands, gasping with fatigue.

The mist cleared, unveiling a hulking black winged creature perched on the table. The shreek continued to grow, swelling and expanding as a spiked tail emerged and its snout lengthened, adding a row of sharp pointed teeth. One leg extended toward the floor; the other kicked the table away, sending it crashing into the wall.

The creature opened one eye, revealing a red stare that was pure evil.

Vertulious stepped closer and reached out a tentative hand to touch the snout. Abigail half hoped the shreek-Omera would leap on the alchemist and do away with him, but it simply butted its snout against his hand. Vertulious smiled, then turned to face the class. "Job well done, Abigail." He clapped, and the class joined in—all except for Endera, who just glared at her.

Cold dread penetrated her bones.

*What had she done?*

# Chapter 3

Hugo hurried up the stone steps of the Balfin School for Boys and pushed open the door. He was late, so the hallways were empty. *Good.* At least no one would pummel him. He made his way to his first class, dreading every step. History had always been his favorite class under Professor Oakes, but the new teacher, steely-eyed Lieutenant DeGroot, continued to find ways to make Hugo's life miserable.

The door to the Assembly Hall opened, and another teacher spied Hugo and beckoned him forward.

"Hurry up, Suppermill. There's a big announcement coming."

Reluctantly, Hugo let himself be pulled in, wishing he had just stayed home. The hall was packed with boys from every year. DeGroot stood up front with his back to the students, busy writing on a board. As Hugo hunted for a seat, someone stuck a boot out, and he tripped, spilling his book bag onto the floor.

Oskar, his biggest tormentor, grinned wickedly down at him.

Laughter rippled through the boys. DeGroot turned, a dark frown on his face. "Silence!"

The hall went quiet.

DeGroot cast Hugo a withering glare. "Suppermill, tardiness is grounds for suspension."

Hugo picked himself up, wanting to tell DeGroot nothing would make him happier, but he caught a warning look from his brother, Emenor, who sat up front. Instead Hugo mumbled an apology and found a seat.

DeGroot must have had other things on his mind, because he turned to face the assembly, clearing his throat and waiting for absolute silence before announcing, "Today, we make history. We have received the go-ahead from the High Witch Council to launch our offensive. War has begun." As excited murmurs spread among the boys, he held his hand up for silence. "One of you boys will be playing a vital role."

Hugo straightened. Boys playing a vital role? The Balfin Boys' Brigade was meant to train them to join the actual brigade once they were of age. Ten-year-old boys wouldn't be much use on the battlefield.

"I'll be needing a cabin boy," DeGroot said. "Someone to look after my weapons and assist me. It's a chance to see the action up close. Who would like to volunteer?"

Oskar leaped to his feet. "Me. I volunteer."

"Me too," another said.

The crowd of boys began shouting and pounding their feet on the ground, all except Hugo.

DeGroot held a hand up, and the boys quieted. "Your enthusiasm is noted. I expected nothing less from my young recruits. I took the liberty of dropping your names in a hat."

He lifted his helmet off the desk and shook it in the air. With his other hand, he made a show of churning the names around before drawing out a slip of paper.

The boys sat forward, holding their breaths as they waited for him to say the name.

"Hugo Suppermill."

There were groans and boos. Hugo sat back, stunned.

"Boys, I want you all to congratulate Private Suppermill." A look of satisfaction crossed DeGroot's face. There was no hint of surprise. Or disappointment. As if DeGroot had *wanted* his name to be chosen. Or maybe . . . had *known* his name would be chosen. Which meant . . . Hugo's name was likely the only one in the hat.

Oskar jumped up. "This stinks. Suppermill's a coward, and everyone knows it."

The boys all grumbled, ready to revolt. DeGroot said nothing, his eyes sliding over to Hugo, challenging him to disagree.

Hugo ignored Emenor's warning glare and stood. "Just because I don't like the idea of war doesn't make me a coward, and anyone who has a problem with that can see me outside."

The room went completely silent. Not even Oskar challenged him.

DeGroot clapped loudly. "I knew you had salt in you. Take your seat, Private. You outrank every boy here. You give the order, and I'll expect them to obey. Now, where were we? Ah, yes, the study of invasions. We have invaded the main hold of the Orkadians, Garamond, several times over the centuries." He turned to the board and motioned with a pointer. "In the past we've had some success with a sea attack followed by a ground army with battalions of the Black Guard and the witches to back them up. But all have failed eventually. I believe this time we have an edge."

"What kind of edge?" Gregor, a boy from Hugo's class, asked.

DeGroot waved the pointer at the ceiling. "The skies. From sea to ground to the air. The Orkadians won't stand a chance."

"How will we fly?" Oskar asked. "Are we going to get wings?"

The boys chuckled, but DeGroot slapped the pointer on the desk, and they snapped upright.

"*We're* not going to fly, fool. The witches will be carried on the backs of Omeras."

"Those beasts will rip us to pieces," Gregor said in awe.

"Not if we control them. Enough talk. Classroom time is over. I want you lined up outside in formation. We will be busy *making* history, not learning about it from books."

The boys spilled out of their seats. Hugo stayed behind until the Assembly Hall was clear, then approached Lieutenant DeGroot.

"Why me?" he asked.

The lieutenant looked up from the papers he was riffling and raised an eyebrow. "What do you mean?"

"Why did you choose me?"

"I didn't. You saw—it was a random selection."

"No. You knew it would be me. Why would you want me?"

DeGroot grabbed Hugo by the collar and hauled him close. "Who says I want you? Someone in high places wants you gone—I'm the one stuck with you."

"Vertulious," Hugo whispered to himself.

DeGroot released him and jerked his head at the door. "Get out. We sail at dawn. You better be there waiting, or I'll hunt you down myself."

Hugo hurried away as icy fear trickled through his veins.

He wasn't going to stop this war.

He was going to be in the thick of it.

# Chapter 4

Abigail lay on her bed in her tiny attic room, staring up at the ceiling. She had loads of homework to do but found she didn't care. Why bother when she was just going to fail unless she did whatever Vertulious asked? He would always be able to threaten her over Hugo. If only her heart really were made of stone, life would be so much easier.

A tap sounded on her shutters. She leaped up and ran to throw them open, expecting to see Hugo, but it was his mechanical bird, flapping its creaky wings. It carried a note in its beak. She pried it loose and quickly read it:

*Meet me by the jookberry tree. Urgent!*

Abigail threw a cloak over her uniform and laced up her boots. The sun was just setting, but with luck, the other witchlings would be busy studying, and she could shimmy down the thick ivy without being seen.

When she arrived at their usual meeting place out of breath, Hugo stepped out from behind the tree.

"I'm sorry about earlier," she blurted out before he could speak. "I don't know why I said those things."

He looked distracted and merely nodded at her words. "It's okay. There's something I need to tell you."

"What is it?"

"I'm being deployed."

"What?" Shock rooted Abigail to the ground. "But how? Has the war begun then?"

Hugo shrugged. "I don't know. I was chosen to be a cabin boy on one of the ships. I'm leaving in the morning."

"No. You can't."

"I just said I am."

"I won't accept it. I'll go talk to Vertulious. He'll listen to me."

He grabbed her arm as she brushed past him. "Abigail, he's the one who arranged it."

She blinked as she took that in. "You know the last three witch details that left haven't come back yet. No one's even heard where they went to."

"So it's up to me to find out what's happening. Remember, I'm a scientist. Nothing bad is going to happen to me."

"How can you be so sure?"

"Because I'm smart. Listen, there's something else. DeGroot said they have Omeras. That they'll be able to destroy the Orkadians from the sky."

Abigail's face flushed with guilt. "Not yet they don't, but they will if Vertulious has his way. He made me use a metamorphis spell in class today, and we turned a shreek into an Omera."

"Why didn't you refuse?"

She bit her lip. "I tried—but he threatened to hurt you. I don't think he really needed me though—he didn't ask me to remove my sea emerald, and my blue witchfire is a lot more powerful." She put her hands to her head. "I don't see any chance of the Orkadians winning. It's all so lopsided without Odin's Stone."

Hugo's eyes lit up. "That's it! What if we found a way to balance the sides?"

"How? It's not like we have a spare Odin's Stone lying around."

"I know . . . but what if we found something to replace it, something equally powerful?"

"Like what?"

Hugo's face fell as he shrugged. "I don't know."

A snap echoed in the swamps.

"What was that?" Abigail asked.

Endera stepped out of the shadows. Her face was pale as snow, her eyes brittle and hard. "Why, Abigail, what a surprise to find you out here plotting against the coven."

Her two cronies, the sturdy Glorian and skulking Nelly, stepped out from behind her on either side. Then a slight figure joined them.

Safina. Once Abigail's friend and protégé.

"She always was a traitor," Safina said.

"Safina, you don't mean that," Abigail said gently.

"Yes, I do." The firstling's eyes flashed. "You let Endera's mother die."

"I didn't," Abigail said. "I couldn't stop it. You were there. You saw what happened."

"Doesn't matter," Endera cut in, "because you won't

be here much longer. I've spoken to Madame Hestera. Told her what happened that night. How you forced my mother to do your work and wouldn't let me save her."

"I did not." Abigail sputtered with outrage, but Hugo gripped her arm.

"What's your point, Endera?" he asked. "If Madame Hestera were going to expel Abigail, she would have done so. Why don't you just leave us alone?"

Endera folded her arms. "I wish I could, but Madame Hestera thought it would be a good idea for me to follow Abigail around. If I can prove she's a traitor, she's promised Abigail will never set foot inside the Tarkana Fortress again. And she will have her magic stripped from her."

Abigail was speechless. Now that Melistra was gone, she had thought she was finally safe. But if Madame Hestera had it in for her, things would be even more difficult.

"Not if I have anything to say about it."

The cool voice came from the edge of the clearing. They all turned to stare as their former Awful Alchemy teacher, Madame Malaria, stepped into view. "Glorian, Nelly, Madame Vex would like some help cleaning the cobwebs from her classroom." The two mumbled something and scurried away. "And you, young Safina." The teacher put a gentle hand on the girl's shoulder. "You are perhaps too hard on someone you once admired. Disappointment can turn a person sour, but perhaps it is yourself you are most disappointed in."

"What is that supposed to mean?" Safina huffed. "I didn't do anything."

"Surely you were the one who told Melistra where Robert Barconian was that night, which led to her taking him. Which led to Abigail coming to the tower. Which led to Melistra's demise. Do not pretend to be innocent of that."

Safina turned ashen.

Madame Malaria faced Endera. "My dear child, I am sure you grieve your mother, but to blame another witchling for Melistra's blind need for power is shortsighted. What good is this vendetta of yours against a witchling who was once your friend?"

"She was never my friend," Endera hissed.

Madame Malaria sighed. "Then perhaps that makes you a good witch, because a witch never trusts anyone. But they do have people they can count on when their goals are aligned."

"Our goals will never be aligned," Endera snapped. "All I want is for her to be gone."

"Oh, pity me, here I thought you wanted revenge for your mother's death," Madame Malaria said dryly.

Endera gawked. "I do, but it's the same thing, isn't it?"

"Is it?" Madame Malaria arched one brow. "Did Abigail steal Odin's Stone? I rather think you helped with that. Did she make your mother go to the fortress that night? No—Melistra arranged that herself. Did Abigail ask your mother to do the job Vertulious asked of her? No—your mother volunteered. So tell me, why do you blame her?"

"Because . . ." Endera looked fit to be tied. "If not for her, my mother would be alive."

"So the fact she was born, which she had no control over, makes all of this her fault?"

"Yes." But Endera looked uncertain, almost confused.

Madame Malaria patted her shoulder. "All I'm asking is that you look deeper into what it is you want—what it is this coven needs—and decide for yourself what the best course of action is." She cupped Endera's cheek. "I am truly sorry for the loss of your mother. Now leave us. I must speak with Abigail alone."

Endera blinked, her eyes bright with unshed tears, then without even glancing at Abigail, she spun and left with Safina chasing her heels.

Hugo shifted on his feet, taking a step back. "I guess I should go too."

The teacher snapped her fingers, halting him. "I heard what you said about finding an object to replace Odin's Stone—one that could save the Orkadians. I think it's brilliant."

Abigail blinked in shock. "You do? I don't understand."

Her eyes darkened with worry. "Unchecked power can only lead to ruin. And with that horrid he-witch in control," she shuddered, "I fear we will burn this world to the ground if we are not stopped. For that reason, I think this plan of yours is wise. And I know just the object you can choose. The hammer of Thor."

Hugo choked.

Abigail's jaw dropped open. "Um . . . that's . . . I mean . . ."

"Not possible," Hugo filled in. "Thor would never let his hammer go to help humans."

Madame Malaria's eyebrow went up. "Have you asked him?"

"No . . . but it's . . . I mean . . . he's Thor," Hugo said. "And Mjolnir is the most powerful object the gods possess. I don't see why he would give it up to help some humans defeat the witches."

Madame Malaria smiled grimly. "It won't be used to defeat us—just to remind my sisters and that he-witch they have much to lose if they pursue this foolish war. We need to restore that balance. Isn't that what you said?"

Suddenly Hugo's idea sounded brilliant. He preened. "Yes."

"But if I go after Thor's hammer, surely I'll be kicked out of the coven for good," Abigail said.

Madame Malaria fluttered a hand. "Oh, you won't be going after the hammer. You'll be going after Hugo to stop him. Tell Madame Hestera what you suspect. Convince her you're the only one who can get close enough to derail his plans."

"What if she doesn't believe me?"

"She might not. But it will make her think twice about rushing into this war—and it might buy some time. She'll be curious enough to send you along."

They stared at the professor, who seemed to have lost her mind.

"This is not going to end well," Abigail said with a sigh.

Madame Malaria shrugged. "No, but it might be our only hope of preventing a terrible outcome set in motion when you brought that vile man back. You must get Thor's hammer and take it to the Orkadians—but be careful who you trust. If they use it against us, this will all have been for not."

"How do we find Thor?" Hugo asked.

Her eyes gleamed. "Rumor is Thor is hunting wild boar in Jotunheim."

"Jotunheim?" Hugo's eyes grew wide. "But that's the—"

"Realm of the giants, yes," she said matter-of-factly.

"But how will we get there?" Abigail asked.

"Word is a certain sailor named Jasper can be hired to do journeys such as this." Madame Malaria clapped her hands. "I must go. Trust in each other and you won't go wrong." The professor snapped her fingers and disappeared in a cloud of purple smoke.

Hugo and Abigail stared at each other.

"Did that just happen?" Abigail asked.

Hugo nodded. "I'm supposed to be deployed in the morning, but instead I'm to go ask Jasper to take me to find Thor to ask him for his hammer to save mankind here in Orkney. That doesn't sound crazy, does it?"

Abigail grinned. "Completely. I'll find Madame Hestera and tell her what I suspect and insist on going along."

"Sounds like an adventure." Hugo's eyes glowed with excitement. "I think I'll pay a visit to Professor Oakes— see if he knows anything about Thor or Jotunheim that might help."

Abigail patted his arm. "Be careful, Hugo. This is a dangerous game we're playing. It could all go wrong. Madame Hestera could have you thrown into the dungeon, or worse."

"I'll be fine. You worry too much. I'll see you in the morning at first light."

Abigail watched him go, unable to stop a tremor of apprehension from running up her spine.

# Chapter 5

As Abigail hurried back to her room, a sliver of hope lodged in her heart. Maybe, just maybe, they would find a way to fix things once and for all. The thought put a smile on her face.

"Don't you look happy," an oily voice rasped.

Abigail jolted to a stop.

From behind a mulberry tree, the familiar figure of Vertulious emerged, as though he'd been lurking there, just waiting for her to come along.

Abigail curtsied. "Master Vertulious, how might I help you?"

He waved a hand. "Call me Verty, Abigail. We are on familiar terms, are we not? What puts that spring in your step?" His eyes probed her keenly.

"I just had an idea how to guarantee I'll be Head Witchling of the secondlings," she rattled off. "Nothing that would interest a master witch such as yourself."

He seated himself on a stump and straightened his robes. "Don't be modest, Abigail. Everything about you interests me. And you're lying," he added, waggling a finger at her. "If you want to be Head Witchling, all you have to do is ask." He snapped his fingers, and a gold T-shaped pin appeared on Abigail's chest. "See? I can make whatever you wish come true. Tell me, what is it you wish?"

He fixed her with a hypnotic stare. She swayed, suddenly wanting to blurt out the truth, but instead she clenched her fists and dug her nails into her palms. The stinging pain snapped her out of it.

She pulled the pin off and held it out to him. "What I wish is to pass all my classes with flying colors—especially Magical Maths, because Madame Vex is so hard. Can you help with that?"

Vertulious stared a moment longer, then his face darkened. "I don't know why you don't trust me, Abigail. I have done nothing but offer my help." The pin in her hand turned to dust.

Abigail choked back her response. Vertulious was a lying, two-faced, power-hungry troublemaker. She bit her tongue and smiled sweetly. "Was there anything else, Master Vertulious? I'm just headed to my room to finish my studies."

He waved a hand, dismissing her. "That will be all. That was fine work in class today," he added as she skipped off. "I can't wait to train our pet Omera to be the leader of our new winged army."

Abigail froze, then turned slowly.

Vertulious stood and moved to stand in front of her, tapping one finger to his chin. "I think I'll capture one of those Omeras you're so fond of. They will be easy to tame, I imagine, especially the young ones. They'll lead us to more of their kind. Yes. First thing tomorrow," he said as if he were talking to himself. He walked off through the trees, leaving her to stare after him.

She wished she could cast a spell to send him to the netherworld, but his powers were too great. Part of her wanted to rush out immediately and warn Big Mama, but her need to give a message to Madame Hestera was more urgent. She would sneak out and call Big Mama later tonight.

Abigail climbed the steps to the tower that led to Madame Hestera's private rooms, then walked down the hall past the dusty portraits of their ancestors. The witches looked down at her with disdain, as if judging her intentions. Outside the door to Madame Hestera's chambers, she smoothed the folds of her skirt with her hands before rapping on the door.

"Enter."

Abigail thumbed the latch and let the door swing open.

The stuffy room smelled of dried herbs. Madame Hestera sat in front of a blazing fire. One hand grasped her emerald-tipped cane. She cast a glance at Abigail, giving a small dismissive sniff. "What do you want, witchling?"

Abigail cleared her throat. "I wanted to speak to you."

"About?"

"Something important. To the coven."

Hestera grunted. "Since when is this coven of importance to you?"

The words were like a lash, stinging Abigail to the core. "Since forever. And I'll prove it. My friend. The Balfin boy Hugo. The one who was there the night Vertulious came back. He's planning something."

Hestera tapped the knob of her cane. "Do you think me a fool? The boy and you share a bond. You would not betray him so easily."

"If he came between me and my coven, I would." Abigail stepped closer. "Whatever you might believe, I am a witch first. Which means my coven comes before everything."

The old witch pursed her pruny lips and then gave the briefest nod. "Fine. What is this boy planning, and why would it interest me?"

"He believes he can stop a war between us and the Orkadians."

A harsh laugh escaped Hestera. "You waste my time. A mere boy cannot stop what is inevitable. You who have witnessed firsthand the power Vertulious wields should know that. With the destruction of Odin's Stone, the Orkadians don't stand a chance."

"What if they had something even more powerful?"

Hestera's grip tightened on the emerald knob. "What. Is. More. Powerful. Than. A. Witch?"

"A weapon of the gods. The hammer of Thor. I think Hugo is going to go after it."

There was silence—the only noise the crackling of the flames. When Hestera spoke, her voice was like chipped ice. "The boy has no hope of finding a god as powerful as Thor, or asking him for his most powerful object."

"That's what I thought. But I think he's hiding something. I don't know what. He's planning on leaving in the morning."

"Then I'll throw him in the dungeons," Hestera said dismissively. "He'll never see the light of day again."

"But what if—" Abigail thought quickly. "What if he's working with others. He trusts me. He thinks I'm on his side."

The old witch's eyes narrowed. "What are you suggesting?"

"That I go with him. Spy on him. See who he's working with and stop him if it appears likely he'll succeed."

"I find it highly suspect that you have had such a change of heart, Abigail. I know the history of your mother. Your unique magic, which you continue to hide. Many thought you were the Curse Breaker until Vertulious came back."

Abigail clasped her hands to keep them from shaking. "Yes, madame, I can't help what I was given or who my mother was. But I can prove my worth to this coven once and for all."

Hestera's gaze drilled into hers. "Do you know what it means to become a witch? It means you must cut out your heart and replace it with hate. You must be molded to fit the needs of the coven, to become a weapon that can be wielded against our enemy. Are you ready for that, witchling? To become a weapon against our enemies?"

Abigail nodded, unable to speak past the lump in her throat.

"Then you can prove it by betraying your dearest friend." Hestera cackled. "That will surely prove the kind of witch you are."

"So I can go with him?"

Hestera drummed her fingers on her cane and then nodded. "I will expect regular reports. My ravens will check in with you. Do not disappoint me, Abigail, or you will find the consequences to be dire."

Abigail curtsied. "Yes, Madame Hestera. I won't let you down."

"And do not involve Calla in this. The girl has a future and a powerful gift of magic, delayed as it was. I won't see her ruined by your foolishness. I intend to see she replaces me one day."

Abigail nodded and slipped out, shutting the door behind her. Her heart hammered in her chest. How was she ever going to pull this off—protect her coven and fix all her mistakes without failing everyone?

# Chapter 6

Hugo rapped his knuckles on the door of the small cottage. The shutters were drawn, and the place had an air of neglect, as if no one had been there in ages. He rapped again, leaning over to peek through one of the slats, but he couldn't make out anything. Maybe Professor Oakes had moved.

Just as he was about to leave, a sudden noise made him stop.

"Psst, Hugo, is that you?" The voice came through a tiny crack in the door.

"Yes. It's me."

"Does anyone know you're here?" The professor widened the door and looked from side to side frantically.

"No. I don't think so."

"Then come in before someone sees you."

The door edged open, and an arm shot out and yanked Hugo inside.

He blinked in the dim interior. He could make out a small sitting area and kitchen with dishes piled up. Books were strewn everywhere, as if an entire library had been tossed on the floor.

Oakes lit a small lantern. "Excuse the mess. I've been doing a bit of research in my spare time."

"A little?" Hugo stepped over a pile of books and followed Oakes into the kitchen.

The professor pushed some books off a chair and motioned for Hugo to sit. "What brings you to my humble abode?" He twitched, hollow-eyed and nervous, as if he hadn't slept in weeks.

"Er, I wanted to see how you were doing."

"Me?" The professor blinked. "Am I okay? You mean after being fired from a job I was exceptionally good at for no reason other than I made a comment that war is an unproductive way to progress?" His voice rose to a high pitch, and he shook himself, settling back. "Sorry, Hugo, I should be more polite to my visitor. What really brought you out this way?"

"I had a question, one I thought you could answer."

"Go ahead."

"What can you tell me about giants?"

"What kind of giants? Orkney has several types. There are the giants that came with the rest of the magic folk when Odin brought the isles here from Midgard. They're puny compared to a real giant. They live up north in a place called Rakim and haven't been heard from in centuries. They call themselves the Vanir, though they're neither frost giants nor descendants of the Vanir gods. They took the name centuries ago because they considered themselves as powerful as the gods and as fearsome as the real frost giants."

"They sound interesting, but I was talking about the kind that live in Jotunheim."

"Jotunheim?" Oakes blinked at Hugo. "You mean giant giants. The kind that are"—he pointed at the ceiling—"as large as the bell tower at school."

"Are they really that big?"

"According to every book I've read. Of course, I've never met one." His eyes narrowed. "Why the sudden interest in Jotunheim?"

"It's for a . . . uh . . . school assignment."

"Well, it's not a very nice place. I think I have a map of it somewhere." He went to his shelves and thumbed through his books until he found the one he wanted. "Here it is." He flipped the pages until he came to a hand-drawn map. "It's mostly frozen over. There's a palace called Utgard, which is made out of carved blocks of ice. The air is so cold your nose will freeze off if you stay outside too long. Not to mention it's infested with all sorts of horrid and unspeakable creatures."

"Creatures?" Hugo immediately flashed back to the viken that had stalked them in the swamps. "What sort of creatures?"

Oakes's lip curled with disgust. "Trolls. They work the forges for the giants to make their weapons. The troll hags roam the woods, setting traps for the unwary passerby."

"Sounds like a nice place to visit," Hugo joked, studying the map. There were mountains. Lots of mountains. And deep forests.

Oakes snapped the book shut. "What is this really about?"

Hugo weighed out what to say. "What if someone were trying to come up with a way to stop the witches from winning this war?"

Oakes hissed, looking around the room as if the shadows hid lurking figures. "That's treason, Hugo. I could be hanged for even discussing it."

"This is just hypothetical. For a class assignment," Hugo reminded him.

Oakes leaned back, folding his arms. "Go on then."

"If one were going to find a powerful object that could stop the witches, or at least slow them down, something like, I don't know, hypothetically speaking of course, maybe something like . . . Thor's hammer . . ."

The professor gasped, one hand going to his mouth. He bit down on his knuckle, then nodded at Hugo. "Go on."

"I was just wondering how one might go about finding it. Or convincing a god like Thor to help out. I hear he often travels to Jotunheim."

The professor's eyes filled with understanding, and he stood, pacing back and forth in the small kitchen. "Hypothetically, of course, there are several ways one could get Thor's attention. He has been known to favor mankind. He isn't the smartest god, but he has a kind heart. He hates giants. Loathes them. Of course, it will do you no good to get his hammer without his Belt of Strength and gauntlets. They're a complete set—can't use one without the other."

"What could we bargain with?"

"As I recall, Thor was once humiliated by the giant king, Utgard-Loki." Oakes pulled down an ancient-looking tome and flipped through the pages. "Here. This is the story. Thor was wanting to test his strength out against the giants, hoping to rid the land of a few of them in the process. He was traveling with the mischief-maker Loki and his human companion Thialfi in Jotunheim when it became dark, and they took shelter in this strange hall. It kept rumbling and shaking. Lo and behold, turned out it was the metal glove of a giant named Skrymir."

"That's a big giant," Hugo said, "if they could shelter in one of his gloves."

"Yes, they're called giants for a reason. In the morning, the giant woke up, and turns out, his snoring was the reason for all the rumbling and earthquakes. Skrymir offered to let Thor and company travel with him, but the next night he kept everyone up with his snoring, so Thor tried to hit him over the head with his hammer. Each time, the giant woke and asked if it was an acorn or leaf that fell on his head."

Hugo's eyes bulged. "Thor hit him with Mjolnir, and it didn't destroy him? I thought his hammer was powerful?"

"It is, but the giant used magic."

Now Hugo was really confused. "The giants have magic?"

Oakes nodded. "A strange and ancient magic they call on to enchant people and confuse them. Skrymir was actually redirecting the blows, which were so hard they created entire new valleys."

"So what happened?"

"The next day Skrymir bade them farewell, and Thor and company made their way to the ice kingdom, where they were greeted by a band of giants in a great hall. The giants' king, Utgard-Loki, welcomed them but said only those that could prove they were best at some sort of skill could stay. Loki went first, bragging he could eat more than any other creature."

"Did he win?"

Oakes laughed, turning the page and pointing at a drawing of a large man devouring a wooden platter. "He finished his plate but lost to a giant who ate not only all the food but the platter as well. Thialfi went next. He was known to be the fastest runner in the land." Oakes turned to the next page, and Hugo saw a picture of a youth gasping as a giant ran past. "Three times he ran the race, and three times he narrowly lost."

"Surely Thor won his contest," Hugo said.

"That's where it gets tricky." Oakes turned the page and showed a drawing of Thor holding a large drinking horn. "Thor agreed to a drinking contest, and they filled a horn with ale, but even with three large quaffs, he couldn't finish it. So Utgard-Loki offered him something even easier—to lift a cat off the ground."

"Is this a joke?" Hugo asked. "How can a god as strong as Thor not be able to lift a cat?"

"Thor was only able to lift one paw."

"I don't understand."

"You will. So then Utgard-Loki offered to let Thor wrestle with an old woman, but as hard as he tried, Thor couldn't throw her."

"He wasn't able to throw an old woman? How is that possible?"

Oakes snapped the book shut. "Because Utgard-Loki tricked Thor. He disguised himself as the giant Skrymir and learned their weaknesses, then used his magical enchantments to best them. You see, Loki went up against Logi, which is the name for fire, and fire consumes everything. And Thialfi went up against Hugi, which is another name for thought. He was racing against Utgard-Loki's very thoughts, and nothing is faster than the speed of thought."

"And Thor?"

"The end of the horn was attached to the sea, so each time he drank, he was literally draining the sea and lowering the tides. The cat he lifted was actually Jormungand, the Midgard Serpent. He nearly dragged it out of its prison."

Hugo was fascinated. "Who was the old woman?"

"That was Elli, old age itself. No one can fight old age. It always wins in the end. Utgard-Loki finally confessed all of this to Thor, which of course made Thor angry—so much so that he went for his hammer, only to find that Utgard-Loki and his hall had vanished."

"That's an amazing story," Hugo said. "But how does it help?"

"Thor has a long memory. He won't have forgotten his humiliation. He might be willing to hand over his hammer temporarily for information on where Utgard-Loki is."

"Thank you, Professor," Hugo said. "I don't suppose you know how to find this Utgard-Loki's castle."

Oakes tapped his nose. "It's not on any map, but I'm sure a resourceful boy could find a way."

# Chapter 7

Abigail hurried out of the gate and into the swamps. It was past supper now—the other girls had gone to their rooms to finish their studies—but Abigail had no intention of doing schoolwork. She would probably never be allowed back in class again, not once she helped put an end to this war. She might as well make the most of her last night, and that meant finding a way to warn Big Mama.

It had been a few months since Abigail had seen the big creature, but she was certain the Omera would still come if she called to it. They had shared a deep connection ever since Abigail had saved her hatchling.

The swamps would be dark and filled with too many slithering creatures for her taste, so she took the path toward Baba Nana's house on the edge of town. It had a nice clearing that Big Mama had come to before. The Omera would be safe there, away from prying eyes, long enough for Abigail to give her the message.

Baba Nana had not been back to the shack since Endera's mother had cursed her with a freezing spell that had left the old woman in a state of near death. She had been moved to the Tarkana Fortress, where Madame Vex cared for her with the help of Calla.

The door to Baba Nana's shack hung half-open on its hinges, and there was no trace of smoke rising from the chimney. Abigail undid her cloak and put her fingers to her mouth, letting out a high-pitched whistle. It could take a while for Big Mama to answer, depending on how close she was. She sat down on the porch, thinking of all the things she needed to do before the morning. What did one pack to go visit Jotunheim? It was cold there, she remembered, but that was all she knew.

A snapping sound in the woods brought her head around. She stood, wondering if it was Big Mama. A small rathos ran across the clearing, and she relaxed. Then a shadow crossed the moon, and she looked up, a grin splitting her face.

Big Mama landed with a *thump*, blowing out a long snort of steam as she stalked toward Abigail, arching her wings up high.

"You came." Abigail ran a hand over the pebbled skin of Big Mama's snout. "How are the babies?"

Next to Big Mama, a sturdy figure with dazzling star-filled eyes landed. "Starfire! It's you!" She threw her arms around the young Omera's neck. "Look how big you are! You've grown three sizes."

The young Omera tossed his head proudly.

"Big Mama, I've come to warn you," Abigail said. "It's not safe for you here."

The Omera's head whipped around to face the trees, and she growled low.

"What is it?"

Suddenly there were witches everywhere, dropping out of the trees and flinging nets over the creatures. Abigail got tangled up in the netting and fought to free herself.

The shreek-Omera they had created in class landed with a *thud*, Vertulious on its back. "Excellent work," he said, an evil smile creasing his face.

Several of the witches carried torches, which cast flickering shadows around the clearing. Abigail made out at least a dozen witches holding down the edges of the nets as Big Mama tried to free herself. Next to his mother, Starfire squawked in fear.

"Tell her to calm down or else I'll eliminate the younger one," Vertulious said.

"No, leave them alone!" Abigail freed herself from the netting and attempted to fling herself at Vertulious, but he held her off with a stiff arm.

"Do it now, Abigail, or so help me, I will incinerate the young one. I don't care, and you know it." In his free hand, he held a glowing ball of deadly witchfire.

Abigail fought back tears, hating him so much. "One day I'm going to destroy you," she said through clenched teeth.

Big Mama tossed aside three witches with an angry rear of her head. The wild creature would soon tear through the netting. If only she could devour this he-witch, Abigail thought, erase all their problems.

Several of the witches called up balls of witchfire, prepared to launch them at the thrashing Omera, but Vertulious called out, "Don't harm her. She's too important—she'll lead us to others. Now, Abigail, call her off. Before it's too late."

Abigail couldn't stop the tears running down her face. She walked up to Big Mama, who glared at her with rage-filled eyes. "I'm sorry. I wanted to warn you. It's my fault. Please stop fighting them, or they'll hurt Starfire."

Big Mama screamed in rage, tossing her head as Vertulious raised his arm, prepared to launch his witchfire at the young creature.

"Last chance, Abigail," he said.

"Please, Big Mama. Please," Abigail pleaded. "Do as he says."

Big Mama slowly calmed down. Vertulious approached her warily. He nodded at the witches, and they pulled the netting free. She reared her head back, snarling at him.

*Eat him*, Abigail thought. *With one bite, tear him apart.*

But the other witches still held Starfire in the nets. Big Mama tossed her head as Vertulious stood before her, waving his hand through the air as he recited a powerful charm spell.

*"Melly onus, stella kalira, demos mora gestera."*

The fire in Big Mama's eyes dimmed like coals going out. Her body relaxed, the steam rising from her nostrils now the only thing moving.

"You see, Abigail, with your help we have returned the Omera to where they belong. Under our control." Vertulious stepped up to Big Mama, put a hand on her neck, and pulled himself up onto her back.

"What should we do with this one?" a witch said, pointing at the whimpering Starfire.

"Bring it," Vertulious said. "It's too small for battle now, but it will grow with the proper training." He kicked Big Mama in the sides, and she took off into the air with a screech. The shreek-Omera snapped at Abigail before following its master.

"We always thought you were a traitor to the coven," the witch holding Starfire said to Abigail. "Tonight you proved you belong. Welcome, sister." She led Starfire off, leaving Abigail shattered.

# Chapter 8

Hugo lay awake, staring up at the ceiling. His rucksack was stashed under his bed—he'd made sure to pack warm mittens and an extra-thick sweater. He'd been nervous at supper, barely able to answer the worried questioning from his parents. Emenor had studied him with those knowing eyes of his, as if he knew what he was up to. Hugo had ignored him, trying to enjoy the farewell supper his mother had prepared, but his stomach had been in knots, and he'd pushed his food around his plate.

He was about to doze off when the face of his brother floated into view.

"What are you up to, you little turnip?" Emenor grabbed Hugo by his shirt and hauled him upright.

"Nothing. What's your problem?"

"My problem is you have a way of getting into trouble, and that affects me. If I hadn't stopped you from standing up for that Orkadian brat, you would have sent this entire family into the streets."

"I wish I had." Hugo hung his head. "I wish I had stood up for my friend, even if it meant everyone else suffered."

Emenor clapped him lightly on the ear. "That's because you're a turnip head. Our mother would never have forgiven you. I would never have forgiven you. So spill it. What are you planning, and why are you dressed?"

Hugo lifted his eyes. Part of him wanted to confess everything, but the other part worried what his brother would do.

"Do not even think about lying to me." Emenor twisted Hugo's shirt until it was hard to breathe. "I've known you since you took your first squalling breath. And I will protect you until you take your last," he added in a low voice. "So tell me what you're up to so I know whether to throttle you myself or let you run off and do something foolish."

Emenor loosened his grip and sat down on the edge of the bed. Pale moonlight came in through the slats of the shutters, striping his face.

Hugo searched for the right words. "Do you think this war is a good idea?"

Emenor shrugged. "War is a way of life around here. I try not to think about it."

"Now who's lying? I know you don't like it. I've seen your face when everyone's talking about it. You're the only one who doesn't look happy."

"So?"

"So what if I could stop it?"

"You?" Emenor laughed. "You're a turnip head, or have you forgotten?"

"Maybe. It's just . . . I have an idea how to make this war go away."

"So spill it."

Hugo told him about their idea to find the hammer of Thor.

"You'll never find it," Emenor scoffed. "And even if you did, he'd never give it to you."

"Says who? The gods have helped mankind before."

"They'll throw you in the dungeons for even thinking this. It's too dangerous."

"That's what Abigail said, but one of the witches, Madame Malaria, thinks it can work."

Emenor's eyes brightened. "Malaria said to give it a go?"

"Yes, she doesn't like Vertulious."

He snorted. "How could she? He fired her—didn't like the competition. So let me see if I have this straight. You plan to try to find Thor, a known giant killer and possessor of the most powerful weapon in the world, and what—ask to borrow it?"

"Something like that. It's sort of a work in process."

Hugo waited for Emenor to drag him out of bed and take him straight to the High Witch Council. Instead, Emenor slumped back, running a hand over his shorn scalp.

"When did you get so grown up? This is a good plan, Hugo. It's crazy, but if it works, it could make a difference. There are those of us who quietly worry about the witches' hunger for power. If that Vertulious gets his way, this world will be nothing but dust and ashes."

Hugo threw his arms around Emenor's shoulders. "Thank you. I promise, I won't let you down."

Emenor patted his head, then held him at arm's length. "How is it Abigail is going to go with you? She's a witch. This will be treason."

"She's going to tell Madame Hestera what I'm planning and ask to come along to keep tabs on me."

Emenor's hands dropped. "She's going to tell Madame Hestera?"

Hugo nodded. "It's the only way she can come along and not be a traitor."

"You little fool," Emenor hissed, yanking Hugo close. "You're going to bring the witches down on us."

"But—"

"No buts. The witches will double-cross you every time. You have to leave. Now."

He shoved Hugo toward the window as Hugo fumbled with his boots. "Why are you so worried?"

"Hestera won't risk letting you go after the hammer. She'll simply eliminate you now and never have to worry about it."

Hugo grabbed his coat and hurriedly buttoned it up. He threw his small rucksack over his shoulder. "I'm sorry."

Before Emenor could answer, a pounding sounded at the front door. Emenor's eyes grew round with fear. "Out the window. I'll try to delay them."

Hugo threw open the shutters. The moon was still up, but a sliver of dawn creased the horizon. He tossed his bag out and let Emenor boost him up and over. He landed in the small garden. Dew crisped the grass, and a small rabbit scurried away.

"Don't get yourself killed," Emenor hissed. "Make sure you come back so I can thrash you."

"I will." Hugo snatched up his bag and gave Emenor a quick nod before darting into the woods.

It was an easy path to the harbor. A thin layer of fog covered the calm sea, draping the ships in ghostly wisps. Hugo slipped onto the decrepit ship that belonged to the crusty sailor Jasper. The deck was deserted, but Hugo wasn't fooled.

A whisper of motion behind him was his only warning before a cold blade settled on his neck.

"Did anyone follow you here?'

"No. I don't think so."

"Then come below before anyone sees us." Jasper

released him and scurried to the hatch, then lifted it and disappeared from sight.

Hugo followed him down the ladder and sat down at the small galley table.

Jasper struck a flint and lit a candle. "I got your note," the sailor rasped. "What kind of trouble are you in now?"

"I need your help," Hugo said. "Abigail and I are going to stop the war."

One bushy eyebrow went up. "The blue witch is working against the witches?"

"No. Well, sort of. We just want to find a way to stop them from going to war."

"The two of you caused enough trouble bringing that Vertulious back."

"It wasn't . . . I mean . . . it probably was our fault. We did everything we could to stop it, but Vertulious—"

"Was far too clever," the sailor finished. "So what's this plan of yours?"

Hugo quickly explained. At the mention of Thor's name, the old sailor snorted with laughter. "You think a little sapling like yourself is going to gain the attention of a high and mighty god like Thor?"

Hugo nodded. "Thor is a protector of mankind, like Odin. If we explain why we need it, maybe he'll help."

"The gods don't have time to interfere with the battles of mere mortals. They've left this place to fend for itself. If it's overrun by the witches and threatens them, you know what they'll do?"

"Yes. They'll erase it. Don't you see? We can't let that happen. Help me. Take me to Thor."

"Take you . . . boy, I don't have access to Asgard."

"He's not in Asgard. Madame Malaria says he's hunting wild boar in Jotunheim."

"Jotunheim." Jasper grunted. "You want me to take you to the land of the giants?"

"Yes. Now, please. Witches were at my house this morning looking for me, and I'm supposed to report for deployment and be shipped off."

"So you've got witches after you, and you're running away from your duties?"

"No, I'm trying to fix things. Will you help me or not?"

"I wish I could, but one boy can't go up against a god like Thor. It will never work."

"What if I went with him?" The voice came from the stairs and Abigail stepped into view. "I'm going too."

"Blue Witch, you can't get involved in this," Jasper said in his gravelly voice. "It's too dangerous. Odin would never approve."

"So don't tell him."

He shook his head. "I don't think you understand."

"I do," she said. "We might not find Thor. We might fail. But we have to try. It's my fault this is happening. It's up to me to fix it."

He eyed her keenly. "What about your coven? This goes against everything. They'll kick you out for sure."

Abigail didn't flinch. "My coven deserves better than someone like Vertulious leading it."

Jasper studied them both, and then the old sailor sighed. "So it's treason, is it? All right then. We best heave anchor before anyone shows up looking for you."

# Chapter 9

Abigail clung to the railing, adjusting to the rolling deck as Jasper's sails snapped in the salty air. For a raggedy ship, it seemed sturdy enough, cutting through the waves as they left Balfour Island behind. She had sailed a few times but only to nearby islands. This was an adventure unlike anything she had ever experienced. Hugo settled into helping Jasper—he had spent last summer sailing on the boat, so he knew it well. Abigail watched enviously as he knotted ropes and pulled in rigging lines like an old pro.

A gust of wind knifed through her, and she shivered, huddling in her heavy cloak.

"Here." Hugo passed her a pair of thick woolen mittens. He wore a similar pair.

She pulled them on gratefully. "Thanks."

"You ready for this?"

"Ready to head to the realm of the giants? No, but I've been worse places."

"At least it's not a den full of spiders," Hugo joked, recalling their time in the netherworld.

"Right, just bloodthirsty giants." She lapsed into silence. Big Mama's eyes haunted her. Vertulious's charm spell had taken away her control—the fierce creature would hate that. And Starfire—the poor thing was probably terrified.

"Is everything okay?" Hugo asked. "You seem sad."

Abigail told him about Big Mama. "I just wanted to warn her, but instead I got her and Starfire captured. Vertulious has placed her under a charm spell so she can't even fight back. I hate myself." Tears stung her eyes and she wanted to scream with frustration.

Hugo put his hand over hers. "Abigail, you couldn't have known Vertulious would follow you."

"He always seems to be a step ahead of me. I think the only reason he changed that shreek into an Omera was to trick me into calling them."

Hugo squeezed her hand. "We'll find a way to outsmart him, I promise."

Abigail turned to watch the rapidly receding outline of Balfour Island. Doubt ate away at her. Was she doing the right thing? Would they even be able to find Thor? What if he just laughed at them?

"He won't," Hugo said firmly.

"Won't what?"

"Laugh at us. That's what you're thinking, right? It's all I think about—that if we do find Thor, which is a big if, he'll just laugh at us."

"So what makes you think he won't?"

"You."

"Me?" Abigail snorted. "I'm not exactly a reason to help. I'm a witch, remember?"

"No. You're the daughter of a friend of his."

Abigail reared back. "My mother did not know Thor as far as I know."

"No, but your father did."

"My father?"

"Aurvendil. Remember the story? Of how his spirit became a star?"

Abigail frowned. "I should know, of course, but there was a lot happening. You said something about a long journey and getting frozen."

"Yes. Aurvendil the Brave was a friend to Thor and traveled with him. When they journeyed across the frozen lands of Jotunheim, Thor carried him in a basket on his back, and Aurvendil's toe froze. Thor threw it into the heavens, and it became the morning star. Thor knew your father."

"Oh." Abigail took a deep breath. "Then that might help. Unless he doesn't like witches."

"No one likes witches," Hugo said with a grin. "But he might like you."

Abigail rested her chin on her hand, staring at the rolling waves. Her nose was frozen, but she didn't want to go below yet. Thor had known her father. Had spent time with him. Maybe he would tell her more about him.

A flickering shadow caught her eye. Two wheeling ravens kept pace with the ship. Her heart turned cold. Madame Hestera was having them followed. They were not on some lark. This was life or death. If they failed, witches would perish. Robert might lose friends.

Abigail turned away from the ravens and went below.

# Chapter 10

*e*ndera stepped onto the deck of the Balfin warship, dressed in black from head to toe. At her side, Glorian and Nelly waited silently, with Safina trailing behind. Honestly, the firstling was a nuisance, but seeing her tagging along never failed to annoy Abigail, so she was worth keeping around.

"Is everything as Madame Hestera commanded?" Endera asked haughtily.

The captain hardly glanced at her. He had a grizzled face that had seen years at sea, and a thin scar ran across his cheek up to the corner of his eye. "I don't take orders from no witchlings," he sneered, turning his back on her. "Get below and stay out of me way."

Endera let her rage burn into a white-hot glow. She raised her hand, calling up a ball of witchfire, and threw it at the man's behind. He squealed in pain as his trousers caught fire, sending him running to dunk himself in a barrel of water as he shouted threats at her.

Endera snapped her fingers, and the man's lips froze. "Do not ever speak to me in such a manner again. I represent the High Witch Council, which you serve. You will do as I say without question, or I will report you to Madame Hestera, and I assure you, she won't just singe your trousers."

The man glared at her, then must have decided it wasn't worth it. He pulled himself out of the barrel and sketched a quick bow. "As the witchling commands." He began snapping orders at the others to haul up the sails. "Where might we be headed?"

"Keep that ship in sight." Endera pointed at the small ship on the horizon.

The captain drew an eyeglass from his pocket and squinted into it. "That scum bucket can't outrun us—we can overtake them in an hour."

"Fool, I don't want to overtake them. I want to follow them. Make sure they don't see us, or you will pay. Lose them, and I suggest you not return home."

He nodded, then whirled away to yell at the sailor keeping watch in the crow's nest to keep an eye on the ship.

"Where do you think she's going?" Safina asked.

"Doesn't matter," Endera said. "It's our job to follow her and report back to Madame Hestera. She's entrusted us with proving once and for all Abigail Tarkana is a traitor to the coven. I look forward to seeing the day she is stripped of her magic."

# Chapter 11

A deep roll of the ship awoke Hugo, nearly tossing him from his bunk. Lightning flashed through the tiny porthole and lit up the cramped cabin. He sat up, putting his glasses on.

"There's a big storm," Abigail said from the other bunk. She was sitting up with her arms wrapped around her knees.

"Where's Jasper?"

"Up top. He said not to come up."

"You think he's okay?"

Abigail shrugged. "He didn't seem bothered. I imagine he's been through storms like this before."

It was their third night on board. The first two days had dragged as the small ship endured endless rolling seas with no sign of land. Thick clouds had turned everything gray. Cold winds had pierced Hugo's coat, chilling him to the bone, and his nose felt permanently frozen, but staying below meant leaving Jasper alone. Hugo wanted to help, and so did Abigail.

Another streak of lightning lit up the sky, and thunder rumbled loud enough to shake the timbers of the ship.

"Is that normal?" Abigail asked.

"I don't know. The storm must be awfully close by."

A sudden dip threw Hugo forward, and this time he hit the floor. Abigail landed on top of him. They untangled as water rushed in at their feet.

Jasper ripped the hatch open. "Need some help."

Hugo and Abigail scrambled up the ladder.

On deck, they held on to the railing as gusts of wind threatened to blow them overboard. Rain lashed Hugo, soaking him to the skin. Lightning painted the sky, hitting the water in endless strikes. Thunder boomed so loud it hurt his ears, and the sea just rolled and rolled, crashing against the side of the boat as though it wanted to break it to pieces.

"Those sea witches don't want us coming in," Jasper shouted. "I'll need your help to steer."

"Sea witches?" Hugo asked.

"Mermaids. They guard the entrance to Jotunheim."

Lightning danced on the horizon, and Hugo saw the danger. Stone spires began rising out of the water, jagged points glistening in the moonlight, just waiting to tear their ship to pieces. Behind the channel, steep cliffs rose straight up.

"Grab the wheel, both of you," Jasper ordered.

They fought their way against the wind, grasping on to the wooden spoked hub.

"Pull hard to the right when I say the word." Jasper made his way to the main sail and began hauling it up. As the wind snapped it full, he shouted, "Now!"

They spun the wheel, forcing the ship into a hard right turn. The ship rolled onto its side as the wind pushed it,

and it narrowly avoided a rocky spire. Jasper shoved on the boom with both hands, pushing the sail to the other side as he shouted at them to turn the wheel back. Their hands slipped on the slick surface as they followed his commands, weaving in and out of the rocky barriers.

A spire rose out of the water directly in front of them. Jasper shouted at them to turn, but they couldn't spin the wheel fast enough. There was a horrible grinding noise as the hull scraped against stone.

And then they were through.

The winds died down to an eerie stillness. The moon cut through the clouds, casting gleaming light across the silent sea. Something ruffled the surface of the water. Hugo caught sight of a silver tail, and then it was gone.

A shiver ran up his spine as more ripples marred the surface.

"I think there's something down there." He leaned over the rail as Jasper shouted at him to stay back.

Too late. A pale arm reached out of the water, grabbed him by the collar, and yanked him overboard. He hit the surface with a splash, choking and gasping as icy water filled his lungs. He managed a breath before another pair of hands latched on to his ankles and tugged him downward. He kicked his legs, trying to break free, but the hands gripping him were like manacles.

His ears popped, and spots danced behind his eyes. His lungs burned with the need for air. And then a bright streak lit up the water, and the creature holding his ankle let out a garbled scream. Abigail snatched Hugo's arm and tried to pull him upward, but the sea witches had other ideas.

They swarmed around Abigail and Hugo, hands grabbing at them, silvery bodies a blur. Several held spiked tridents that looked sharp enough to pierce armor. Then suddenly the mermaids let go, retreating back to form a circle around them. One mermaid swam forward, her long red hair flowing behind her. She offered them each a prickly sea cucumber with a strange mouthpiece made of carved shell and gestured to put the opening to their mouths.

Abigail put her lips around it and then turned to Hugo, shoving the odd thing to his mouth.

*Breathe*, she motioned to him.

*What's the point?* Hugo thought. The sea cucumber wasn't going to breathe for him. They were going to die, here under the water. He only wished he could have said a proper goodbye to his parents.

Abigail punched his arm, and he dragged in a breath, prepared to gag on seawater, but instead, precious air filled his lungs. The shell sealed around his mouth in a tight suction, and funny little tentacles tickled his lips. The sea cucumber was like a filter, dragging in water and sending out tiny air bubbles. It made a gurgling sound when he inhaled, but if he took shallow breaths, there was air.

Another mermaid swam up and put his glasses back on.

The red-haired mermaid beckoned them to follow. Two grabbed Abigail and Hugo on either side, pulling them along with powerful flips of their tails. Now that Hugo could breathe, the scientist part of him wanted to see everything. Glowing tendrils of kelp rose from the seafloor, casting a neon-green light that bathed the schools of colorful fish and seahorses swimming around. A snapping eel poked its head out of the seaweed, revealing spiny teeth, and then retreated when the mermaid jabbed her trident at it.

Abigail nudged Hugo's arm and pointed. Up ahead, a dome rose from the seafloor, growing larger as they drew near. Inside, an underwater city sparkled in the dappled light with flashes of pink coral and gold-tipped spires.

The mermaids swam through a small round opening and popped up on the other side in a shallow pool. As they stepped out of the water, their tails divided into two legs; the scales faded, leaving only faint ridges along the backs of their arms and legs. Attendants waited with robes, which the mermaids knotted around their waists.

Hugo surfaced next to Abigail, pried loose the sea cucumber, and took a deep breath. They climbed the steps, handing the sea cucumbers to the waiting attendant.

"Are you all right?" Abigail shook the water out of her hair.

Hugo wrung out his shirt. "Fine. What is this place?"

The mermaid with red hair spoke up. "Welcome to Zequaria. I am Amarina. Come, our queen awaits."

"Who is your queen?" Hugo asked.

"Queen Capricorn, the most powerful creature of the seas."

Hugo frowned. "What about Aegir? Isn't he the god of the sea?"

Amarina whirled, poking a finger in his chest. "Do not speak that name again if you wish to keep breathing."

Abigail put a hand on his arm. "We're sorry. We won't do it again."

Amarina led them down a path lined with rock ponds. Pink starfish and giant red lobsters crawled in one. In another, a purple octopus looked up at them with one eye before darting away to hide in a small grotto.

Mermaids clustered in small groups, whispering to each other, eyeing the two kids with curious looks.

"Why are there no mermen?" Hugo asked.

"Our queen does not permit it," Amarina said. "You are the first male to step foot in Zequaria in centuries."

The path wound among small buildings all made of pink coral. It ended in front of a tall structure much grander than the others. Instead of coral, tiny shells inlaid into the plaster made this building sparkle. Twin spires rose up to the ceiling of the dome, their tips dipped in gold. Amarina led them up a broad set of polished alabaster stairs into an entryway two stories tall. A chandelier made of conch shells hung from the ceiling. Amarina knocked lightly on a set of double doors before opening them into a spacious round room.

A mural made of inlaid sea glass depicted a large green snake wrapped around the entire room. Where the tail met its mouth, it had swallowed it. In the center of the room, a woman with emerald hair sat on a large throne carved out of whale bone. Two mermaids stood guard on either side, gripping tridents with wicked sharp points. The woman wore a mother-of-pearl crown that glittered with precious stones when she moved. She was beautiful, but her eyes were hard as venadium steel.

"My queen"—Amarina bowed low—"I present to you the children we rescued in the sea. Children, this is Queen Capricorn, ruler of the seas and supreme leader of all sea creatures."

"Tell me your name, child." The mermaid queen ignored Hugo and spoke directly to Abigail.

Abigail dipped into a curtsy. "Abigail Tarkana, Your Highness."

The queen's eyes lit up. "Ah, the sea has brought me a gift," she said, smiling. "Calista has spoken highly of you. She says you possess a strange magic."

"Calista spoke of me?"

The queen fluttered a hand. "I hear things. Tell me, this Vertulious, is he as powerful as they say?"

"Powerful and perfectly awful."

"How is it he came to leave his spellbook?"

Hugo spoke up. "We unlocked the magic in Odin's Stone. He was able to perform a transformation spell with its power."

"I see." The queen drummed her fingers on the arm of her throne. "Do you think he could be put back into the spellbook?"

Abigail frowned. "I don't see how. I threw it into the sea."

Capricorn snapped her fingers, and a young mermaid hurried forward with a tray covered in cloth. She pulled the cloth back, and Abigail gasped. "That's his spellbook. How did you find it?"

"What falls into the sea belongs to me," Capricorn said airily. "You didn't answer my question. Could he be sent back into his spellbook?"

Abigail looked to Hugo. "I'm not sure how."

"He put himself there once," Hugo said. "I imagine he could do it again, if he had no choice."

"Interesting." The queen waved the book away. "Tell me, children, what do you want in the land of the giants?"

"We wish to ask Thor for his hammer," Hugo answered, "to stop the witches from going to war."

The mermaid laughed. "The god known as Thor will not help mere children such as you."

"I am not a mere child—I am a witch." Abigail drew herself up. "And a descendant of Aurvendil, who was known to Thor. I will make my case, and I will get his help."

The queen eyed her for a long moment, weighing her words. "So you wish to fight against your own kind."

"No, I wish to stop them from doing something so terrible that there is no coming back from it."

The queen leaned forward, her eyes calculating. "You will go against this Vertulious, will you not?"

"If I have to."

She settled back on her throne, a satisfied look on her face. "Fine. I will grant you safe passage, but I require payment."

"We have no money," Hugo said.

The queen shrugged. "Some things have great value and are worth nothing. Give me your most prized possession, and you may pass."

"Here." Abigail dug into her pocket and pulled out the small crystal. "A teardrop that belonged to my mother."

"Abigail, no," Hugo said. "You can't."

Capricorn leaned forward, pinching the small stone and holding it up to the light. "Yes. This will do nicely." She took off her crown and pressed the stone into an open spot. It sunk into the smooth surface, winking as the light caught it. She replaced her crown. "You will be returned to your ship. But I fear you will not succeed. In the end, your bones will end up in my sea."

# Chapter 12

Daylight was just forming when Abigail bobbed to the surface next to Hugo. They swam to the side of the ship, eager to get out of the chilly water, as the mermaids left with a flash of their tails.

"So you survived." Jasper grunted, tossing them each a blanket.

"B-b-barely," Hugo said through chattering teeth. "I th-th-thought we were g-g-goners."

"The mermaids were actually nice," Abigail said, shivering. "Their queen, Capricorn, agreed to let us pass."

"You had to give her your mother's teardrop," Hugo reminded her.

"Mermaids are evil creatures. Don't ever trust one," Jasper said. "They have a heart colder than that of a witch, and making trouble's in their blood."

Jotunheim loomed in front of them. Stark cliffs lined the shore—impossible to scale. Snow-capped mountains rose beyond them, disappearing into the endless gray clouds that surrounded the island. The only access was a narrow channel that led inland, carved by a dark river that flowed into the sea.

"Do you think it's as cold as it looks?" Hugo asked.

"Colder." Jasper hauled the sails up. "One moment you'll be talking about the weather, and the next you'll be frozen solid as a statue, waiting for a spring that never comes."

The ship listed heavily, but it made its way slowly upriver. Chunks of ice floated past, bumping against the boat. After a while, the chunks got so thick it became hard to move forward. The boat slowed until it finally came to a stop.

"That's as far as she'll go," Jasper said. "The ice is too thick. If we keep going, we'll be stuck here forever."

"You need to turn back," Abigail said. "Take the boat downriver until we're ready to return."

Jasper frowned. "I can't leave two younglings alone in this wild place. The giants will have you for breakfast."

"We're not helpless," Abigail said. "I am a witch, and Hugo is very capable. If we don't have a boat, we can't leave."

Jasper studied her for a long moment and then scowled. "I suppose you're right. But I don't like it. If Odin hears of this—"

"He won't," Hugo said, "because it's going to be fine. Right, Abigail?"

"Right. Take the boat downstream, and we'll send a signal when we've got what we came for."

Jasper laid a hand on her shoulder. "Good luck, Blue Witch. This ain't going to be easy."

Abigail and Hugo climbed over the side of the ship, and Jasper lowered them onto a sturdy ice floe. They raised a hand in goodbye, then turned and began to walk upriver. At first they had to hop from floe to floe, but soon the ground had frozen solid, and it was easier to make headway. The walls on either side were slick with ice-covered stone.

"How long do you think it goes on like this?" Abigail asked.

"I don't know, maybe forever."

She elbowed him. "Not funny."

"A little funny. I think we'll get there soon."

"Why do you think that?"

"Because I see a bridge."

He pointed at the way ahead. Sure enough, the chasm was crossed by a stone bridge that spanned both sides of the river. Frozen moss and green algae glistened through the ice.

"How do we get up there?" Abigail asked.

"I think we might be able to climb." Hugo felt along the wall. "Look here—the walls are made of clay. Someone's chiseled holes, like handholds."

"I'll go first." Abigail hoisted herself up the first step. "I think this will work," she said as she reached for the next hole.

They climbed steadily, their breath steaming in the air.

Abigail was near the top, reaching for the ledge, when something popped out of the wall right in front of her face. It was an animal with white fur and a round head at the end of a long narrow neck. Its sharp little teeth nipped at her wrist. Startled, she screamed and drew her hand back, losing her grip.

She scrabbled to find a grip. "Hugo, hang on!" she called, and then a strong arm reached out and grabbed her wrist. Below her, Hugo grasped on to her ankle, and they dangled in midair. With a loud grunt, their savior hauled them atop the ledge.

They turned to find themselves staring down into the face of a stalwart bearded figure no bigger than a child.

"You're not a very big giant," Hugo said.

"Giant?" The bearded figure laughed. "I hardly think anyone's ever called me that. Name's Rego. I'm a dwarf, in case you haven't noticed."

"I'm Hugo, and this is Abigail."

Rego sketched a bow. "Pleasure to meet you both. I thought you were goners there."

"We would have been if you hadn't grabbed on to me." Abigail rubbed the red mark on her wrist. "Something came out of the wall and bit me."

"A hoblet, most likely," Rego said with a grunt. "They like to burrow and nest in the cliffs. They're pesky little vermin—they'll steal you blind if you're not careful."

Abigail took a good look around. Snowy blankets draped towering trees, and icicles hung from their branches like pointed teeth. Snow began to fall, fat flakes that drifted down and clung to her lashes. An icy wind whistled through the trees, and she shivered, feeling the chill deep in her bones. "Is it always this cold here?"

Rego laughed. "This is a summer's day compared to some, little lady."

"I'm not a little lady," Abigail said haughtily. "I am a witch."

Rego grew still, staring at her as if she'd grown an extra head. That probably wasn't the smartest thing to admit, she realized, since no one in Orkney particularly liked witches.

But Rego merely said, "Witch or not, you'll be needing shelter. Come along, I don't want you freezing to death and having the witches blame poor Rego."

The dwarf set off, jauntily forging a trail in the snow. Abigail and Hugo tried to keep up, but they were panting and heaving before long.

Rego stopped in front of a fat tree and knocked sharply on the trunk. A small knot slid to the side, and a whiskered face stared out. Then the knot slid closed, and a hidden door opened, spilling out light and welcome heat. Rego hurried inside. Abigail and Hugo followed, shutting the door behind them. They descended down a few short steps into an underground room, where a fire crackled in the small hearth. A pair of dwarfs sat on mushroom-shaped stools, while another stirred a pot hanging over the fire.

All three stopped to stare at the newcomers.

"Who's that?" one of the dwarfs asked, eyeing them suspiciously from under bushy black brows. "And why'd you bring them here? We're on a secret mission. They could be working for the giants."

"Do they look like they work for the giants, Obie?" Rego tugged his boots off and warmed his toes by the fire. "That one says she's a witch." He jerked a thumb at Abigail.

The dwarfs gasped, drawing back. Abigail and Hugo took the opportunity to inch closer to the fire.

"Thanks for letting us stay here," Hugo said.

"Stay here?" Bushy-Brows puffed. "No one said they could stay here. Rego, you've gone too far. If they find out—"

"They're not going to find out unless you flap your trap," Rego said.

"Find out what?" Hugo asked. "Maybe we can help."

"Nothing!" they all said in unison.

"Well, it's obviously something," Hugo said.

In the silence that followed, Rego cleared his throat. "We haven't even made proper introductions. Abigail, Hugo, that sourpuss over there is Obie." He pointed at Bushy-Brows. "The ugly mug with the shaggy hair is Mullet." Mullet raised his hand half-heartedly. "And our chef and host is Pipps over there. Pipps lives here year-round, though how he puts up with the cold is beyond me," Rego grumbled.

Pipps was the cheeriest by far, with rosy cheeks and a twinkle in his eye. He waved a wooden spoon. "You children hungry?"

Hugo's stomach rumbled loudly, and Pipps chuckled. "Sit, sit at the table. Rego, get them a bowl, and I'll serve them some of my jackrabbit stew."

Abigail took a seat on a hard stool, suddenly starving. She spooned a bite from the bowl Rego set before her, savoring the rich, meaty taste. Hugo did the same, and in a few short minutes, they'd cleared their plates.

"I see you like my cooking." Pipps swooped their dishes up. "Put some meat on those bones before the giants devour you." He chuckled again, and the others joined in.

"Ignore Pipps," Rego said. "He likes to have himself a good laugh. So tell us why you're really here."

"Well," Abigail said, "we're curious to know more about giants and the ones that, um . . ."

"Hunt them," Hugo added.

"Hunt them?" Rego's brow went up. "There's only one person fool enough to hunt a giant, and that'd be the god of thunder himself, Thor."

"We've heard about Thor," Abigail said. "It would be an honor to meet him. I don't suppose you know where we can find him?"

"Find him?" Rego sputtered with laughter, and the others joined in. "You're not serious, are you? Two children such as yourselves meeting the mighty god Thor? You'd have a better chance getting an audience with Odin."

"I've already met Odin," Abigail said haughtily. "I think Thor will speak to me. He was a friend of my father's."

Rego's laughter died. "Then tell us, child, who was your father?"

"Aurvendil."

The room grew silent.

Rego's lips pursed. "Don't lie to us, witchling. We know your kind. And you're no descendant of Aurvendil the Brave."

Abigail lifted off the emerald necklace she always wore and handed it to Hugo, then conjured up a ball of blue witchfire. "Do you see this? It's witchfire. If you know anything about witches, you know it's always green. But mine is blue. You know why? Because my father is a star. The morning star. The same one that used to be Aurvendil."

The dwarfs stared at her, whispering among themselves.

"Any witch can conjure up strange magic," Obie said.

"Obie's right," Mullet said from behind the shaggy fringe that covered his eyes. "Why should we believe you?"

Abigail sagged, letting her witchfire die. "You shouldn't. It's too fantastic. I met him once. So did Hugo."

"He was really kind." Hugo passed her necklace back to her. "He had golden hair, and he told Abigail to trust her heart as her guide."

"No disrespect, but it's a mite farfetched." Rego twitched his whiskers. "How can a star descend from the sky?"

"How can Thor toss his big toe up and turn it into a star?" Abigail countered. "My mother used to walk along the shore, watching the stars. He said he fell in love with her."

"Hold on," Obie said. "There's no witch that has a heart in their chest. It's nothing but a cold stone."

"No, my mother was different, or at least when she met him, she changed. He was allowed a few days away from being a star." She fingered the pendant. "I've had to hide my magic with this sea emerald I got from an old sailor named Jasper."

"You know Jasper?" Rego asked. "Well, why didn't you say so?" The dwarf seemed to relax a bit.

Abigail leaned forward. "Then you'll take us to see Thor?"

Rego hesitated. "Thor is rumored to be hunting boar in a nearby valley. I suppose it couldn't hurt to pass by."

"What about our . . . you know . . ." Mullet waggled his eyebrows. "Secret mission."

"It's as good as any direction to look for the fool."

"Now see here, Rego." Obie bristled. "We got our own business to take care of."

Rego stared him down. "And we'll take care of it, Obie, in due time. A little side trip won't dent our cause."

"What exactly are you doing here?" Hugo asked. "I mean, seeing a band of dwarfs in giants' territory seems rather . . ."

"Odd?" Rego filled in. "You think we're in over our heads?"

The others snickered at his joke.

Hugo smiled but pressed on. "You didn't answer the question. Why are you here?"

The troupe fell silent, exchanging wary glances.

Rego tossed another log on the fire. "What you want with Thor is your business, and why we're here, I reckon that's our business."

"And that's fine," Abigail said. "We don't care what you want with the giants. We just want to find Thor and ask him for his—"

"Advice," Hugo cut in. "You know, about how Abigail can remember her father."

"Right. Advice," Abigail said. "Any memories that he had."

Rego looked between them and then grunted. "I don't like it, but we're not going to leave two children on their own, not in this dangerous land. You know what a giant looks like?"

"No," Hugo said, "but I imagine they're big."

"Aye, and strong enough to toss you clear across the sea, but they're not the worst thing out there."

"And what would that be?"

"Troll hags. If you come across one, run. They're worse than the giants, and twice as likely to run your head up on a pike."

# Chapter 13

They slept around the small hearth in the base of the tree. Cold seeped through the ground, making it impossible to get warm, even though the fire put off a nice heat. As daylight made its way through a small window cut high into a knothole, Abigail opened her eyes, rubbing away the grit. She'd barely slept, and her body ached. She longed for some fresh air. Tossing aside her blanket, she tiptoed past the sleeping figures and climbed the small wooden steps to unlatch the door.

Outside, a fresh layer of snow covered the ground. The trees looked as if they had been painted with thick white brushstrokes. She stomped her feet and walked among the bushes, running her fingers over icy clumps that then drifted to the ground.

A furry round face popped out of the leaves. It was brown with a white stripe that ran down its long neck. She smiled. "You're a hoblet, aren't you?"

It chittered back, eyeing her curiously.

"Don't bite me now." She stretched her fingers out, and it let her scratch its chin. Then, before she could blink, it

ran up her arm to the top of her head, tugged on the red
ribbon that tied her hair back, and pulled it free before
dropping to the snow.

"Hey, give that back, you little thief."

It darted away into the bushes. Before Abigail could
give chase, a harsh sound made her stop.

"*Cacaw*!"

Abigail turned to find a large raven perched on the
branch of a low tree. Its feathers were a shiny blue-black,
but its eyes glinted green.

"I am Bristle," it rasped. "Have you a message for my
queen?"

"Madame Hestera?"

The raven nodded.

"No . . . yes . . . only that we're going to find Thor."

"Then you'll get rid of the boy?" Bristle stretched its
neck toward her, tilting its head to the side.

Abigail's heart clenched. "What? No! That's not
necessary."

The raven hopped closer. "Madame Hestera says it is. If you want to remain a witch, you best mind your ways." It sprung up, flaring its wings in her face and scratching her cheek with its sharp talon before climbing into the sky.

"Does he know?" The voice came from behind her.

Abigail whirled around, one hand flying up to the stinging cut.

Rego stared accusingly at her.

"Know what?" she asked.

"That you're betraying him."

"I'm not. It's complicated. Hugo is my friend."

"Friends come and go. To a witch, the coven always comes first."

"Well, I'm not just any witch."

Hugo's head popped out of the trunk. "Abigail, there you are. Why are you bleeding?"

Abigail glared at Rego, then brushed past him. "I scratched myself on a branch. We should be going. We've wasted enough time." Her heart was still pounding in her chest. She would never hurt Hugo, not even if her entire coven depended on it—but things were getting more and more complicated.

The other dwarfs tumbled out after Hugo, bundled up in woolen scarves and fur-lined boots. Obie scowled at her, scratching at his beard. Mullet shook his bushy hair out, clapping his hands together and blowing on them. Pipps handed Abigail and Hugo matching woolen caps that covered their ears.

"Watch out for hoblets," he said as he waved them off. "They'll steal every scrap of food and leave you to starve."

Rego hoisted his pack and began striding through the woods. "Keep up," he called over his shoulder. "We don't have time for stragglers."

Hugo and Abigail hurried after him.

"Where are we headed?" Hugo asked.

"North. To the Three Valleys," Rego said without breaking his stride.

"Three Valleys?" Abigail asked.

"The ones Thor made when he threw his hammer at a giant," Mullet answered. "It's a good story if you haven't heard it."

"I know it," Hugo said excitedly. "The king of the giants disguised himself as a giant named Skrymir and tricked Thor into thinking his hammer was like an acorn falling on his head. But really, he used magic to send the hammer flying past him, and it hit the ground so hard it made all new valleys."

"You know your giant history," Mullet said, sounding impressed. He glanced over at Abigail. "I never met a real witch before. I half expected you to have horns. You look . . . well . . . ordinary."

"Not all witches are bad," Abigail said, "although I suppose most are."

"You have some sort of code," he said. "Your hearts are made of granite."

She laughed. "A witch's heart is made of stone," she corrected. "Cold as winter, I cut to the bone."

"Sounds pretty bleak."

"Abigail's not like the others," Hugo offered. "She's nice."

"No such thing as a nice witch," Obie grumbled from behind them.

"Obie's right." Rego stopped to catch his breath. "A witch'll turn on you when you least expect it, stick a knife right between your ribs with one hand while she's shaking your hand with the other." His eyes met Abigail's, as if he was daring her to admit her guilt.

Abigail glared back at him. "I would never hurt a friend. Ever."

He harrumphed and continued on.

They lapsed into silence as the trail wound uphill; it was hard to walk and talk at the same time. Their breath frosted in the chilly air. Abigail's feet felt like blocks of ice in her boots—what she wouldn't do to soak them in a tub of hot water.

Finally Rego raised a hand, calling a halt. He stood at the edge of a shallow hole that was longer than Abigail was tall and half again as wide. "Giant tracks."

"That can't be real." Abigail eyed the crater. "That would mean the giant was . . ."

"About average sized for a giant," Rego said. "Passed by not long ago. Best lie low."

They continued on, edging around the footprint. Here and there, splintered tree trunks blocked their way, as if something large had snapped the trees like twigs.

Suddenly a loud *crack* split the air, followed by shouts and the sound of thrashing in the snow. And then a boy broke out into the clearing.

A familiar boy with a sheaf of brown hair, dressed in a leather tunic.

Robert Barconian.

"Giants!" he yelled as he burst into their group.

"Robert, there you are." Rego grasped his shoulders. "We've been searching high and low for you."

"No-time-giants-right-behind-me," he gasped out. "We need to go, now!"

Then he saw Abigail and Hugo, and his face hardened. "What are they doing here?"

"Wait, he's your secret mission?" Abigail asked.

"They're looking for Thor," Rego said.

"Well, they're traitors." Robert pointed at Abigail. "She's a witch, and he's a Balfin, which makes them both enemies. Leave them for the giants. Now, before they come."

But it was too late. A pair of trees came crashing down right next to them, hitting the ground with a loud *thwack*, and then the face of a giant appeared over their heads. Its eyes glimmered angrily as they landed on their small group.

"There's that thieving rat," it said. "The king of giants wants your head."

A large meaty hand flew down toward them, aiming to crush their group.

"Run!" Rego shouted, shoving Abigail and Hugo out of the way.

The giant's fist splatted into the icy drift where they'd stood, spraying them with powdery snow.

Abigail picked herself up and threw a ball of witchfire at the giant's face. The blast hit the giant square in its nose, and it roared in pain, swinging another meaty fist down at her. She dove to the side, barely dodging it.

"Let them fight the giant," Robert said. "They can distract him while we get away."

Rego stood uncertainly.

"You work for my father, which means you must do as I say," Robert ordered. "And I say she's a traitorous witch. Leave her to the giants the same way she left me."

"Robert, no," Abigail said. But the giant was coming around for another attack. She had to focus on defending herself and Hugo. He had his medallion out and was using it to call up a windstorm, sending flakes of snow swirling into the air. The giant got confused, stomping in the wrong direction.

Hugo grabbed Abigail's arm. "Come on, before the giant can see again."

"Where did Robert go?" Abigail turned every which way, trying to see in the near whiteout. "I can't believe he left us."

"Oh, believe it," Hugo said, dragging her away. "I don't think he remembers us very fondly."

# Chapter 14

Abigail huddled in the small cave where she and Hugo had taken shelter, really nothing more than a tumble of rocks pushed together. They had a small fire thanks to her witchfire. The crackling flames melted the layer of snow off her and into a puddle, but inside, she was frozen.

Seeing Robert had been hard. He was so angry. Not that she blamed him, but she had tried. Tried to do the best she could. She had saved him. Didn't that count for anything?

Hugo tossed another stick in the fire. "He can't stay mad forever, you know."

"Says who?" Abigail said glumly.

"Says me. We can apologize, but it's up to him to forgive us. I think he will."

"What is he even doing here?" she asked. "Do you think he ran away?"

"You don't suppose . . . ?"

Their eyes met across the flames. "He's after Thor's hammer," Abigail said with sinking dread. "Of course. He must have realized the same thing we did—it's the only thing powerful enough to stop this war."

"What if he doesn't want to stop it?" Hugo asked.

Abigail frowned. "What do you mean? Of course he'd want to stop it."

Hugo shook his head. "Think about it, Abigail. He's pretty angry. He thinks we betrayed him."

"Why would he want Thor's hammer if he doesn't want to end this war?"

Hugo's face was grim. "What if he does want to end it—with the Orkadians winning and the witches losing."

Abigail's breath rushed out of her. "You mean destroy us."

"It's possible, right? If he gets hold of Thor's hammer, he could give it to his father, and he might—"

"Wipe us out," she finished. "We'll always be a threat to the Orkadians. Hugo, this is a disaster."

"No. We just have to make sure he doesn't get his hands on it first."

"But . . . ugh!" She leaped to her feet and began pacing in the small space. "It all feels so wrong. He should be helping us. The whole point was to convince my coven not to go to war because the Orkadians could defend themselves with the hammer, not actually use it against us."

"I don't think he sees it that way."

"Then what do we do?"

Hugo blinked. "I'm not sure. We should probably find Thor, and fast."

"Even if we find him, how are we going to get him to give us his hammer?

"We need something to bargain with." Hugo pulled his notebook out and leafed through it. He tapped a page. "Professor Oakes said the king of the giants, Utgard-Loki, bested Thor in a battle of wits. Thor's never been able to get revenge because Utgard-Loki uses magic to move his palace and hide it."

"And?"

"And if we can locate his castle, maybe we can use that to get Thor to give us his hammer—at least long enough to stop the war."

"And how are we going to find a magical moving palace?"

"I suppose we have to find a giant and get taken prisoner."

Abigail blinked at him. "Are you serious?"

"Yes."

"That's a terrible idea."

"Have you got a better one?"

She sighed, folding her arms. "No, but that doesn't mean I like it. Either we stay here and freeze or get thrown in a giant's dungeon." She kicked dirt over their small fire. "Might as well get started. If Robert gets to Thor before us, freezing to death will be the least of our worries."

# Chapter 15

*e*ndera stepped onto the block of ice and studied the footprints. "I believe they went that way," she said, pointing upriver. Glorian and Nelly stepped down next to her, followed by Safina.

Endera turned toward the ship, which floated next to the ice floe. "Captain, I command you to tie off and send a group of your men with me."

The captain nodded, tugging on his cap. "Aye, aye, madame witchling. Just give me a moment to organize the men."

Endera turned back to studying the tracks. "With any luck, we're not more than a day behind. If that stupid captain hadn't been so afraid to come in past those wretched stones . . . Sailing around them cost us precious time."

"Er, Endera, why's the ship going that way?" Glorian asked.

Endera spun around, enraged to see the ship sailing away.

"Hey, get back here!" She threw a ball of witchfire straight for the captain's head, but it fell short and sputtered out in the water. The ship kept going. Endera caught a glimpse of the captain at the helm, bowing slightly. One of his men tossed a bag over the side, and then the ship turned the corner and was gone.

"He left us." Endera could hardly believe her eyes. "That little sea rat left us. When I get back, I'm going to turn his bones into soup. I'm going to curse every member of his family for generations. I'm going to—"

"Endera," Nelly said. "I d-d-don't want to complain, but it's f-f-freezing cold." The girl's lips were already a shade of blue.

"Oh, stuff it," Endera said. "You're a witch, aren't you? Conjure up a spell to keep warm."

Nelly called up a ball of witchfire, and the other girls held their hands over it to warm themselves.

"Safina, go get that bag. Maybe the captain left us some supplies."

The witchling scrambled over the ice, grabbed the bag, and dragged it back to where they stood.

"Open it," Endera commanded.

Safina undid the buckles and opened the duffel. It contained nothing more than the cloaks they'd brought on board.

Endera dropped to her knees and pushed the cloaks aside, rummaging in the bag. "Tell me he left us some food . . . Ugh!" She pounded her fist in the snow. "There's nothing useful in here."

"Everyone, take your cloak," Safina said calmly. "That's something—it will help us stay warm."

Glorian and Nelly eagerly wrapped theirs around their shoulders.

"You think a cloak is going to stop us from freezing once the sun goes down?" Endera snapped. "A cloak isn't going to stop the cold sapping the life out of our bones."

"Don't be so dramatic," Safina said. "We just need to find shelter."

Endera glared at her. "We're on a frozen river. Have you seen the cliffs rising up on either side? The captain left us here to die."

"Which we're not going to do," Safina said. "Abigail would have found a way. We just have to follow her tracks, and we'll get off this river."

Endera's rage spiraled higher and higher until she wanted to explode. Glorian was shivering. Nelly looked terrified. Safina was the only calm one. And suddenly, that made Endera calm.

"Don't tell me what to do, firstling. Obviously I was going to follow Abigail's tracks. I was just pointing out that if we don't get moving, things will get bad." She pushed past the girl and began stalking along the ice, scouring the ground for clues as to where Abigail had gone. There were different sets of tracks, as if more than one group had passed through here, but all of them headed upriver.

She spied a smallish boot print and knelt, running her fingers along it. It had iced over, but it left the strangest feeling. As if it belonged to someone she knew. A friend.

"What is it?" Nelly blew into her hands. "You see a way out of here?"

"No." Endera stood. "It's nothing."

As if a witch ever had friends, she reminded herself. She refused to think his name, but a face with a sheaf of brown hair floated into her mind, and a half smile crossed her face.

# Chapter 16

Hugo didn't want to complain, but he couldn't feel his toes. Or his knees, for that matter. The snow was so deep they kept breaking through the crusty surface and sinking up to their waists. And the white stuff was still falling—as if the sky held an endless supply. His chest burned when he breathed in the frigid air, even though he was sweating with the effort of plowing forward.

"Abigail, I'm sorry . . . I just need . . . to rest," he puffed.

"Not much farther, Hugo," she said, stubbornly wading on. "We just have to get to that rock over there. If we climb on top, we'll be able to see a long ways."

The rock was just visible through the trees, perched atop the hill they had been steadily climbing.

Hugo sighed as he slogged after her. "It's going to be dark soon. If we don't find shelter . . ."

"I know, we'll freeze," she said over her shoulder. "Really, Hugo, you should find something original to say."

"It's just that I don't want to freeze to death."

"And I said we'll find shelter as soon as we get to the top of that rock." She pointed at the large boulder. "We'll be able to see everything from there. Maybe we'll see where this giant's ice castle is."

"Or maybe we'll see more trees and snow," Hugo muttered.

"I heard that."

"Well, it's true."

"Why are you always so negative?"

"I'm just being logical. The odds are that all we'll see is what we see now—trees and more trees."

"The giants have to live somewhere, which means cities. Big ones, I imagine. So if we get to the highest point, don't you think it's possible we'll see signs of them?"

Hugo stopped, gasping for air. "You're right. I'm sorry. I'm just—"

"Tired." Abigail blew on her hands. Frost crusted her eyelashes, and her cheeks were chapped and red under her wool cap. "So am I."

"You don't look it."

"Because I can't give up, can I? If Robert gets to Thor first, we'll have to stop him. And I don't want to do that."

"I know."

"So we have to find this giant's lair and then bargain with Thor for his hammer. Otherwise I'll never be able to fix all the mistakes." A tear slipped from her eye and quickly froze on her cheek before she turned and continued on.

"None of this is your fault," Hugo called after her. "Vertulious had centuries to make his plan."

She stopped, her hands fisting at her sides. "I know. I still should have seen what he was really up to."

Hugo waded to her side. "How? You're only a secondling. You don't even have all your powers."

"I had enough to help Vertulious, didn't I?" she snapped back, and then immediately her face changed. "I'm sorry." She put a hand to her head. "Every time I remember that night, I just . . . I can still hear his voice. It's like the spellbook still has its hooks in me."

"Is that why you threw it into the sea?"

She nodded grimly. "Yes. To be sure it could never come back."

"Why do you think Capricorn wanted it so badly?"

"I don't know." She turned as a twig snapped loudly nearby. "Did you hear that?"

"Yes, probably just an animal. I've seen hoblets running around."

"That was too big for a hoblet. Show yourself," she called, conjuring a ball of witchfire. "Now, before I burn this entire forest down."

"Don't hurt us," a voice whispered timidly. "We means you no harm."

A pathetic-looking creature peered around the trunk of a tree, then stepped into view. Frizzled hair poked out of a threadbare cap, and ragged clothes covered her stout figure. One snaggletooth poked down over her bottom lip, and her eyes bulged, rolling in different directions as she studied them. "You seems too smarts to be out in this cold," she said as she shuffled closer. "Izmerelda doesn't thinks children should be out here alls alone."

"Who's Izmerelda?" Hugo asked.

"I's Izmerelda." She got close enough to poke a finger at Hugo. "Aren't you a strapping boy? There's meat on them bones."

She chuckled, but Hugo saw the flash of malice in her eyes. He took a step back. "Abigail, I think these are the troll hags Rego warned us about."

Abigail hefted her ball of witchfire. "Get away from my friend or find out what a witch can do."

But before she could launch her attack, a clump of snow dropped from the tree overhead, burying her witchfire as more of the creatures sprang from behind trunks. Two of them grabbed Hugo, wrenching his arms behind his back, while two more took hold of Abigail. Worse, a pair of snarling animals prowled out of the bushes, heads lowered as they bared sharp fangs. They looked like a cross between a small bear and a wolf, with stocky brown bodies, rounded ears, and a mask of silver-tinged fur around their eyes.

"Ties them up," Izmerelda ordered her fellow hags. "There's a hefty bounty to be's collected."

"What bounty?" Hugo asked as one of the awful-smelling troll hags bound his wrists with cord.

"The one ons your head." She pointed a crooked finger at him. "The son of Odin. Robert Barconian. You's stole something that belongs to the king of giants himself."

Abigail started to argue. "He's not—"

Hugo elbowed her. "That's right. I'm Robert Barconian. I demand you take us to the giant king."

"R*iii*ght," Abigail said, catching on. "The giant king who's in his magic palace. That's who we want to see."

The troll hag sneered, her lips peeling back to reveal blackened teeth. "Then you's a bigger fool than you's look. Utgard-Loki likes to bake the bones of children in his bread." She cackled with laughter, and the other crones joined in. "And if he finds out this one's a witch, he'll string her up by her toes."

"What does he have against witches?" Abigail asked.

"He's superstitious, he is. A witch washed ashore here once. One of Utgard-Loki's uncles captured her, and she hexed him with a spell that turnt him the size of a troll—and not a big one, minds ya. Now the mere mention of a witch makes the king scairt. No giant wants to be small."

The troll hags marched Hugo and Abigail to a large sled piled with pungent animal pelts. Two of them led the beasts to their harnesses. "Get ons, unless you wants to walk," Izmerelda snapped. "Or I can feeds you to my badgets. They's always ready to eat."

The beasts looked at them over their brawny shoulders, a thin stream of frozen drool hanging from their jaws.

Abigail and Hugo clambered atop a pile of skins, ignoring the rank odor. Izmerelda let out a shrill "*Hiyaka!*" and the badgets lunged forward. The sled rode easily atop the snow, careening back and forth as the animals nimbly wove between trees. Hugo thought for sure he and Abigail were going to tumble out, but the other troll hags clung to the sides, leaning just far enough to keep the craft from flipping.

"This is a bad idea," Abigail whispered to him. "I don't like it one bit."

Hugo sighed but said nothing. There were so many things that could go wrong with his plan he had stopped counting.

When they crested the hill, a pristine white plateau lay before them. Hugo groaned. He'd been hoping to see signs of a city, but there was just snow and more snow. The troll hag stopped the sled, traced a small circle and then an X in the air with one crooked finger, and whispered strange words.

A shimmer swept across the snowy field. As it passed, a ripple appeared in the air, as if Hugo were looking through a soap bubble. Then it cleared, revealing the most amazing sight.

A glistening castle rose before them, every facet glittering in the afternoon sunlight. It looked as if the entire

thing had been carved of ice. Even the wall surrounding the castle was made of carved ice blocks.

Abigail's jaw fell open. "Is that—"

"The city of the giants," Hugo supplied, thinking it was the biggest city he had ever seen.

Izmerelda snapped the reins, urging the badgets on. The sled raced across the field toward a pair of iron gates, the only thing not made of ice. Two giants stood on either side, each holding a lance as thick as a sapling and as tall as the giants themselves. Their leather tunics were trimmed in fur, and weapons were strapped to every inch of their torsos.

One of them squatted down to get a closer look at the sled. Scars crisscrossed his forearms, and his nose looked as if it had been crunched in a fight.

"Aye, troll hag, what are you doing with these puny scraps? You know His Highness doesn't like humans."

"These isn't just any humans," Izmerelda said. "This is a son of Odin." She pushed Hugo forward. "There's a bounty on his head. His Highness wishes to see him."

The giant sniffed at Hugo, unconvinced, then turned to study Abigail. "This one smells of magic. She's not one of them witches, is she?"

"Of courses not," Izmerelda lied. "We knows how the king feels about witches."

"She's my healer," Hugo said. "She travels with me. A son of Odin would never consort with a witch."

The giant stood. "You may pass, but expect no favors today. His Highness is in a foul mood."

Izmerelda scratched her chin. "Why is that?"

"Thor has returned to the land of the giants."

Hugo looked at Abigail. So Thor really was here. That was a good sign. "How do you know?" he asked.

The giant swiveled to look at him. "We have eyes everywhere. Thor should know to stay away." He waved them through the gate.

Izmerelda drove the sled under a towering blue arch. The buildings were so tall Hugo had to crane his neck back to see the tops. Giants lumbered about everywhere. The females looked as fierce as the males, sporting weapons and flexing muscles as they pushed and shoved each other about, as if it were a sport.

The air smelled of burning steel and ash. They passed by blacksmith shops with sweating trolls working iron forges while others pounded hammers on molten metal, making giant-sized weapons. The male trolls were even uglier than the troll hags, with blunt noses, sneevil-like tusks poking up from their lower jaws, and a pair of short horns on either side of their heads.

The trolls stopped their work as the children passed, eyeing them as if they were sizing them up for their stew pots.

"Really. Bad. Idea," Abigail muttered.

# Chapter 17

The tight ropes chafed Abigail's wrists. When they got out of this, she was going to give Hugo a piece of her mind for having the worst idea ever. Until then, she had to keep her witch wits about her.

They left the blacksmith shops behind, and the street widened, leading toward a colossal building capped with four ice-blue turrets. For all its size, it was only one story—the giants were too big and heavy to have a second floor, she guessed.

Izmerelda turned the sled away from the double doors guarded by two fierce-looking female giants and went down a narrow side alley, stopping in front of a troll-sized side door. She stepped off the sled and hauled the children up, dragging them forward. The troll standing guard outside barred their way.

"And where does you thinks you's going, troll hag?" He glowered at them from under bristly brows. His lower tusks jutted up, and his horns, though short, were pointed and sharp.

"Move aside, Ozzie. I'ves got business with the king." She gave Hugo a shake. "This one took something from His Highness." She tried to move past, but the troll guard shoved her back.

"Don't care if he's the king's own offspring—he wants no visitors today. We can throw him in the dungeons till the king's ready to see him."

"She'll share the bounty with you," Abigail said quickly. "The bounty on his head. It's large. Right, Izmerelda?"

The troll hag snarled at her but shrugged. "I reckons I can spare a few coins."

"I wants half." Ozzie's eyes lit up greedily. "Or he can rot in the dungeons."

"Half is fine," Abigail said.

Izmerelda growled deep in her throat but nodded. She waved at the other troll hags to follow, but Ozzie held his hand up. "Just you. Those others smell like they ain't bathed in weeks."

"Go on then." Izmerelda shoved Abigail and Hugo inside.

The corridor was lit by small torches and sized for trolls—the children had to bend their heads to avoid the ceiling. At the end, Izmerelda stopped and turned to them. "Don't speaks to His Highness unless he speaks to you first. Don't looks at him. Don't embarrass Izmerelda, or she'll boil your bones in stew herself. And whatevers you do"—she stabbed her finger into Abigail's chest—"don't let on you's a witch, or he'll boil us both in hot oil." She turned and opened the door.

They stepped into the biggest room Abigail had ever seen. Fur pelts had been strewn over the ice floor. A fire roared in a stone hearth, but it didn't seem to stop the cold. Giants sat around a long table in the center of the room, arguing and shouting.

Izmerelda shoved them toward the table. It was two times as tall as Abigail's head. Conveniently, a small set of steps led to the top. They made their way among the dishes and past towering shakers of salt until they reached the end.

A giant with cinnamon-red hair and a long beard sprawled back in a throne made of pointed ice crystals that fanned out behind him. He brooded over a large tankard cradled in both his hands.

"Your Highness." Izmerelda dragged out a long bow. "We brings you the brat you have been searching for."

At her words, the giant's head snapped up, interest lighting his eyes. "You brought me the Son of Odin I seek?" His hand swooped down on Hugo, grasping him by the back of his collar and lifting him to his face. "Where is it, boy? Where is my treasure?" He blinked. "This is not the boy who stole from me."

The giant tossed Hugo back onto the table, where he landed with an *oof.*

Fear passed over Izmerelda's face. "Course this is hims—we tracked him through the woods. Robert Barconian. Tell him, boy."

Hugo got to his feet. "I . . . I'm not him. Sorry."

She glared at him, then her eyes lightened. "Maybe he knows wheres to finds him. We could torture him. Get hims to talk. My husband is a right good torturer, Your Highness."

The giant king mulled it over. "Fine. Get him to tell you where my fjalnar is, and I'll pay you twice your weight in gold."

He dismissed them with a wave of his hand. Izmerelda gave Hugo a shove, but Abigail had heard enough.

"Stop!" she shouted, witchfire springing to her hand. "You will not harm a hair on him. He is a Balfin, and he is under my protection."

There was a collective inhale of fear around the table as giants stumbled backward, several drawing weapons but most looking too afraid to do anything more. Utgard-Loki took refuge behind his ice throne.

"You brought a witch here?" he roared at Izmerelda. "You traitorous troll hag, you'll rot in my dungeons for that."

"I'm sorry, Your Highness," Izmerelda wailed. "I thought you would want to lock her up."

"I'll toss her into the deepest pit we have and bury her with stones—that's what I'll do," he said.

"Not before I singe that beard off your face!" Abigail waved the witchfire.

"Hold on," Hugo said, getting between them. "What if we could help you get this, er, fjalnar back?"

"And how would you do that?" Utgard-Loki asked from behind his throne.

"We know where the son of Odin is headed."

The giant warily poked his head out. "Tell me and I'll spare your life. You can live out your years rotting in my dungeon, but the witch will be thrown off the highest peak."

"Not before I melt this palace into a puddle." Abigail called up a second ball of witchfire in her other hand.

"Look, just hold on," Hugo said. "Abigail, put the witchfire out."

"No, I told you this was a bad idea. We need to get out of here."

"We need his help," Hugo said. "Besides, I'm hungry, aren't you?"

The smell of roasted meat had been making Abigail's stomach rumble since they'd entered the room.

"Can we just sit down and talk?" Hugo asked. "I promise Abigail won't do anything. She's actually a very nice witch. Right, Abigail?"

"Not today I'm not." But she let the witchfire burn out.

Utgard-Loki rose from behind his throne and straightened his tunic. He sat back down, keeping one eye on Abigail. Hugo sat cross-legged on the table and pulled Abigail down next to him.

"Leave us," Utgard-Loki ordered, and the room cleared of giants, none of whom seemed too interested in lingering with a witch in the midst of them. Utgard-Loki shoved a plate of meat toward the children, and Abigail and Hugo each picked up a sliver. It was tender and juicy and . . . possibly the most delicious thing Abigail had ever tasted. Her empty stomach rumbled in appreciation.

"What's so important about this fjalnar?" Hugo asked between mouthfuls.

"What's so important?" The giant's face turned red. "It's only the most valuable possession I have. A necklace made of bones from Ymir himself."

Abigail nearly choked on her food. "Ymir? You don't mean the creator of the cosmos?"

Like everyone in Orkney, Abigail knew the story of Ymir. Before gods like Odin came into being, the very first creature to have life was a giant named Ymir.

Hugo jumped in. "They say when he died, he spit out the sky. His hair became the trees; his bones, the mountains; his sweat and blood, the seas."

The giant nodded. "That's right. My forefathers harvested some of his teeth and formed them into a necklace. I call it my fjalnar. It means 'little deceiver.' Without it, I have none of my magic."

"What if we could get it back for you?" Hugo asked.

"How?"

"Thor is here, is he not?"

The giant's eyes narrowed. "So?"

"So why do you think he's back at the same time your fjalnar was stolen?"

Utgard-Loki went completely still. "What are you saying, boy?"

"We heard a rumor that Thor paid a boy to . . . uh . . . steal your . . . fjalnar . . . so Thor can get revenge."

Utgard-Loki slammed his fist down on the table, making them jump. "That pathetic god would never dare step foot in my palace again, not after how soundly I defeated him. Did he tell you of our last encounter?"

"I've heard the stories," Hugo said. "How you disguised yourself as a giant named Skrymir and Thor tried to smash your head in to stop your snoring, but each time you enchanted him and deflected the blows."

The giant chuckled, pointing a stubby finger. "Created three new valleys with his blows."

"Then you tricked him into trying to finish a horn of ale, only it was attached to the sea."

"Nearly beached my ships," he said, "the tide dropped so low."

"And then you tricked him into picking up a cat that was actually the Midgard Serpent."

"Aye, that was a close one." Utgard-Loki chuckled. "I thought for a minute the serpent was going to swallow the entire world, until he let it go."

"Lastly, you had him wrestle an old woman who was actually old age, which no one can defeat."

"Hah. I can't help it if the fool didn't know who he was wrestling. Fine." Utgard-Loki sat forward. "You know so much. Tell me why Thor would be foolish enough to return to the place where he was humiliated?"

Hugo grinned. "Because he is a god. A very proud god. He won't let that stand forever. He will want to be remembered as the god who defeated Utgard-Loki."

"Never." The giant roared, leaping out of his seat and smashing his fist down on the table so hard it made the table bounce. "That golden-haired gnat shall not best me."

"Fine. Then you won't be afraid to face him?" Abigail said.

"If he is foolish enough to show his face, I will invite him to supper and feast on his bones."

"But without your fjalnar, how will you defeat him?" Hugo asked.

The giant slumped, rubbing at his long beard. "You make a good point. It's not Thor I fear but that cursed hammer of his. He's unbeatable with it."

"Look, the whole reason we came here was to steal Thor's hammer," Abigail admitted. "We need it to stop the witches from going to war with Orkney."

The giant squinted at her. "I thought you were a witch."

"I am."

"A witch who would betray her own kind?"

"I see it as helping them make better choices." Abigail served herself another slice of meat. "What if we could steal Thor's hammer and get your fjalnar back?"

Utgard-Loki sat back, looking dazed. "Now, why would a witch help a giant out? Your kind has never been a friend to mine."

"Maybe it's time to change that," she said. "If you let us go, we will find a way to get Thor's hammer and retrieve your fjalnar. I give you my word."

He scowled. "Why would I believe a witch? They lie and deceive at every turn. It's in their blood."

"True, but I also have the blood of a hero running through mine. My father was known to Thor—a brave warrior named Aurvendil. Thor turned part of him into a star. I know it sounds fantastic, but it's true. I swear on his life."

The giant studied her for a long moment. Abigail held her breath, waiting to see what he would decide.

Finally, he harrumphed. "You're a strange one for a witch. I don't know why I believe you, but I do. Izmerelda, show your worthless self."

The troll hag, who had been hiding behind a saltshaker, moved into sight and bowed low. "Yes, Your Highness. Izmerelda is here to serves you."

"You will keep an eye on things and ensure the safe return of my fjalnar, or I will pluck your eyeballs from your head personally."

Izmerelda bowed again. "As Your Highness wishes." She sounded completely unexcited. "The trolls are at your command. We serve you. You are our knight."

"Be gone." He waved them away.

They made their way down the corridor toward the exit—but Izmerelda took a sharp turn. "Not running into that thieving troll," she muttered. "He'll wants payment just for using the door."

They came out another entrance to an alley piled high with bins of kitchen rubbish. The smell of rotting meat and vegetables made them gag. They plugged their noses, and hurried after Izmerelda as she weaved between bins to where the sled waited. It had been unloaded, and only two troll hags lingered. Izmerelda drove the sled out of the palace gates and across the field to the edge of the woods. Abigail looked over her shoulder. Behind them, the glittering ice palace shimmered and then vanished, leaving no trace behind.

"Where to, witch?" Izmerelda said, drawing the sled to a halt.

"My name is Abigail."

"Whatever you say, witch. Which way?"

"Do you know the way to the three valleys Thor created with his hammer?" Hugo asked.

"Do I knows my way? Do you's think I'm daft as a giant? I've been all over this ice bucket. Hold on—if you falls out, I'm not turning back for you."

Abigail gripped the side of the sled as the troll hag shouted, "*Hiyaka!*" at her badgets to get them moving. They growled a low *arooo* and began racing across the snow. Wind whistled past her ears.

"Do you think she knows where we're going?" Hugo asked.

"She better."

"And do you think Thor will be there?"

"No idea."

"Do you think we'll get there before Robert?"

"Hugo, just stop. I can't think right now. I have no idea what we're doing, and if I think about it too much, it makes my head hurt. You heard Utgard-Loki. Everyone can see I'm betraying my coven by doing this."

"So what are you saying?"

"Nothing. It's just hard. I want to be loyal, and I want things to turn out right."

"I don't know if that's possible."

"Well, then, if I can't make things right, I just don't want to make them any worse."

"If we can stop this war, we can stop things from getting worse, and maybe things will go back to normal."

"But if Vertulious is still there . . ."

He squeezed her hand. "We'll find a way to get rid of him."

Something in Abigail relaxed. "Do you think that's possible? He ate the apple—isn't he immortal?"

"Not exactly. The apple extends the life of the gods, but they have to eat a fresh one every day. Iduna went missing once, and the gods got terribly sick. Don't you see? He's not immortal. He had just enough power to come back, but he's not going to be here forever."

A sliver of hope ran through her. "Then he might be gone one day."

Hugo nodded. "Unless he can find more of those apples, Vertulious will age and get old and be gone."

Their eyes locked, and they both smiled.

"Right. One thing at a time," Abigail said. "First we find Thor before Robert does and get him to give up his hammer."

The sled rocked hard to the side, nearly tossing them out. "First we have to survive this sled ride," Hugo moaned, but Abigail couldn't hold back a grin. Icy wind whipped her hair back from her face, but she didn't even notice the cold, dreaming of the day when Vertulious was no more.

# Chapter 18

ndera's nose was cold. Her fingers were cold. Her feet were cold. Every part of her was, well, cold. The wind pricked at her ears, slipping under her collar to race icy fingers along her spine. She stamped her boots and blew on her hands. Next to her, Glorian shivered.

"S-s-s-so, End-der-der-aa, wha-what's the p-plan?" The witchling's lips were blue, and her hair was clumped with ice.

"You know the plan. We follow Abigail."

"But the tracks . . ." Nelly's words died at Endera's glare. The skinny witch looked miserable, shoulders hunched under the cloak she had pulled over her head.

The tracks were the problem.

They had followed Abigail's steps to the iced-over bridge. Endera had sent Safina up the cliff first. The girl had climbed it quickly, calling down to them to be careful not to spook the animals that lived inside the holes.

At first it had been easy following the narrow trail through the woods, but the snow had kept falling, and now they were in a vast sea of it. White. Pristine. Unmarked.

"Which way do we go?" Nelly asked. "If we stay out here, we'll freeze. And we've got no food."

"Quit your bellyaching," Endera snapped. "We're witches. We don't complain."

"Honestly, Endera, I would think you'd at least worry about food," Safina said.

The firstling hadn't complained once, which annoyed Endera. Safina should be crying in her boots. It was cold, and they were practically starving.

"Nelly's right. If we don't eat, we won't have the energy to call up witchfire to heat ourselves, and we'll freeze. Is that what you intend?" Safina waited for her to answer.

Endera whirled on the girl. "No, it's not what I intend. I intend to make Abigail pay for what she's done."

"Great," the witchling said without blinking. "Then tell us how we can eat. We haven't seen her or caught up with her in two days."

"I . . ." Endera blinked as a raucous *caw* broke through the clearing. They raised their heads as a large raven settled on a branch to study them.

Endera picked up a chunk of snow, ready to hurl it at the little beast, when it opened its beak.

"Pathetic," it rasped.

Endera froze, letting the snow drop. "Who are you?"

The raven puffed up its feathers. "I am Bristle. I work for the queen of the witches."

"Hestera?"

The raven bobbed its head.

"She's no q-q-queen." Nelly sneered, but her teeth chattered as she said it.

"Ah, but she will be," the raven hissed. "First things first, you worthless half-wits must do your job."

Anger lit a fire within Endera, and a ball of witchfire appeared over her hand. "Who are you calling half-wit?"

The raven stalked closer. "You, witchling. You waste time wandering in circles in the woods while the blue witch marches ever closer to the prize."

"The prize?"

"The hammer of Thor."

"The what?" Glorian blinked her snow-clumped lashes.

The raven cawed with impatience. "Listen, fools—the mission has changed. Madame Hestera wishes that you bring her the mighty Mjolnir."

Endera gaped. "But . . ." *Did the raven just suggest* . . . "That's impossible." The witchfire died in her hands.

"And yet the blue witch plans to do it," the raven hissed, stepping along the branch until it was eye to eye with her. "She has reported her plans to me—she is on her way to meet with Thor, retrieve the hammer, and then she is to get rid of that Balfin friend of hers. But Madame Hestera doesn't trust her. Can you do as asked, or should we find another witchling?"

"Yes." Endera gathered herself. "Tell Madame Hestera I will do as she asks—but how will we return with it? Our captain abandoned us."

"A ship awaits due west of where you'll find the blue witch." The raven launched itself into the air. "Be sure to get rid of her and that companion of hers," it called as it wheeled into the sky.

"Why does she want the hammer of Thor?" Safina asked.

"I don't know," Endera snapped. "But it doesn't matter. If she wants it, it's our job to get it."

"But aren't you curious?" Safina persisted. "It would help to understand why."

Endera had reached her limit with the insolent firstling.

She poked the girl hard in the chest. "You're not in charge here. I am. So unless you have something useful to say, *be quiet*."

Safina pulled back. "You know, you don't know everything."

"I know more than a dumb little firstling." Endera pushed past the girl to stalk on. "Like I know where to find us some food."

"Food?" Glorian suddenly snapped awake. "Now we're talking. Jookberry pie? Shreek pudding? Or maybe some black cabbage casserole?"

Endera rummaged in the snow where the tip of a bush poked through and pulled up a fistful of frozen gilberries. She shoved them into Glorian's hand. "Here. Now quit your yapping and get moving. We have to find Thor."

"And how're we going to do that?" Nelly asked as Endera strode ahead. "You've led us into the middle of a forest with snow in every direction."

Endera stopped, her voice colder than the wind that nipped at them. "You doubt me?"

The girl cringed. "No."

Endera grabbed Nelly by the collar, witchfire appearing in her hand as she hauled the girl close. "Just say it, 'I doubt you, Endera.'"

Nelly held her hands up in defense. "I didn't mean it. I'm just cold. And hungry."

Endera held the witchfire a moment longer and then let it die. She pointed at the sky. "See those vultures? They're following something. Thor is a hunter. I think he's found something to hunt. Follow me or stay here. I don't care." She let go of Nelly and marched on.

One day she would lead the coven, she reminded herself. It would start here. Now. With these three witchlings.

She refused to look back. Refused to show weakness. Glorian would follow her, for sure. And probably Nelly. But Safina . . . She wasn't sure, and she didn't care. And yet she did.

Endera kept walking, and after a few beats, the heavy crunch of snow sounded behind her.

Definitely Glorian.

Then other crunches, lean and sly.

Nelly.

It took a moment, but then, finally, she heard a soft step.

Endera couldn't stop the smile. The witchling had followed. She would come around. She would be Endera's greatest follower.

# Chapter 19

Snow. Snow everywhere. Abigail would have blasted witchfire to melt it all if she could. Her bones ached from the sled's jolting. They had made only two stops to water the badgets and feed them chunks of frozen meat, which the creatures gulped down in one swallow.

"Are we there yet?" Abigail asked Izmerelda for the tenth time.

"Stop pestering me," the troll hag snapped. "I've gots to feed my pretties." She stopped the sled and hopped off to tramp through the snow. "Ah, here we go." She held up a trap. A frightened hoblet quivered inside. Its forehead had a white spot, and its eyes looked out imploringly.

"You can't feed them a hoblet," Abigail said, jumping off the sled.

"Whys not?" The troll hag looked at her as if she'd lost her mind.

"Because they're . . . I don't know . . . not for trapping. Let it go." She raised a ball of witchfire.

The troll hag growled but opened the trap. The hoblet raced away, a brown dash in the snow.

"Don't blame me if'n the badgets take a bite out of your arm," Izmerelda said nastily.

"How much farther is it?" Abigail sighed and dropped the witchfire in the snow, happy to see it melt a hole.

"We're nearly ats the first valley, but it's a fool's journey. You don't even know if this Thor wills be there."

"I think he'll be there," Hugo said.

"What makes you so sure?" the troll hag spat.

"Because of those." He pointed at the sky.

Carrion birds made a lazy circle over the valley below.

"Vultures." Izmerelda snickered. "You think the great and mighty Thor is lying dead?"

"No, I think he might have found some boars to hunt," Hugo said. "It's all we've got. I say we head that way."

Izmerelda pursed her lips. "That way's impossible."

"Hey, the king told you to take us to Thor, so let's go," Abigail said.

Izmerelda bared her teeth. "Watch it, little witch, or you'll find yourself in a hole so deep it will take them weeks to fish you out."

"She just means it's important to the king, so please, show us the way," Hugo said.

"Fine. I'll shows you."

They got back on the sled, and Izmerelda turned and drove the badgets through the trees in the direction they wanted. Eventually they broke out into the open, onto the banks of a river that flowed across the snowy divide.

The scent of rotten eggs made Abigail wrinkle her nose. "What is that smell?"

"That there's the river Elivagar. It's pure venom saids to be milked from the serpent Jormungand before it was caged by Odin in its underwater prison. None cans touch it and live. So cross it if'n you like. I'm staying put." She sat down in the snow, crossing her arms and tucking her chin in. Her two silent companions sat on either side.

"Utgard-Loki told you to stay with us." Abigail didn't like the looks of the roiling dark river one bit.

"He's not here, is he? Nothing's going to makes me get into that river. They'll be fishing your body out downstream."

Hugo and Abigail walked to the bank and studied the current. "Any ideas?" she asked.

"Izmerelda is right. We can't swim across it. We have to find another way. What about using your magic?"

"My magic is useless unless I can turn you into an Omera." Abigail kicked at the snow. "Face it, Hugo, it's hopeless."

He continued staring at the water. "If only there was a bridge . . ."

"But there isn't—" and then an idea popped into her head. "Of course, a bridge! That's it, Hugo! You're brilliant."

His face flushed with pleasure. "What did I say?"

Abigail spun around and paced back toward the edge of the woods. She craned her neck back to stare up at a tall tree, then turned to study the other side of the river. "Do you think it's tall enough?"

"Tall enough for what?"

"To reach the other side, silly."

"I think so. But how are we going to cut it down?"

"We're not. I'm going to use witchfire to burn it down."

Hugo frowned. "But the tree will catch fire."

"Not if you put it out with snow."

"I guess it's worth a try."

Abigail took her gloves off, blowing on her hands to warm them. "Here we go." She shot a stream of witchfire at the base of the tree. Smoke curled up, and then flames licked at the bark. "Snow, Hugo."

Hugo pelted the trunk with snow, snuffing out the creeping flames as Abigail kept up a steady stream of witchfire. Chunks of glowing red embers fell to the ground, sizzling in the snow. Smoke filled the air, stinging Abigail's eyes.

"Keep pelting it," she called as more flames sprouted.

"I can't keep up," Hugo said as the flames grew larger.

"We're almost through." She stepped to the right, making sure to cut around the back side of the tree. "When I say go, we push it over."

Abigail blasted until the last of her witchfire was depleted, then dropped her hands. "Go!"

They ran at the tree, pushing at the blackened trunk with both hands. Heat seared Abigail's face.

"It's not working," Hugo said.

"Push harder."

They grunted, throwing all their might into it, but the trunk wouldn't budge. And then another pair of grimy hands joined theirs. Izmerelda stood beside them, adding her bulk. Finally, the tree gave way with a loud *crack*. They stood back as it slowly fell and landed with a loud *thud*, neatly crossing the river.

"We did it," Abigail said, breathless.

"We better hurry," said Hugo. "The current is strong. I don't know how long it will last."

"Are you coming?" Abigail asked Izmerelda and her two troll hags.

Izmerelda eyed the tree warily. "I reckon it's safe enough, but you's go first to be sure."

Abigail climbed up on the trunk and pulled Hugo up behind her. They stepped carefully, weaving between branches. Water pushed up against the log, making it unstable. Her foot slipped, and Hugo grabbed her arm as she tilted sideways.

"Careful," he said, steadying her.

"I've got it."

The troll hags followed in a line. Izmerelda was the last to step on. As Abigail approached the other side, the top of the tree slipped sideways. Behind them, one of the troll hags shrieked. Abigail whirled in time to see the hag flail her arms, grabbing at the other one next to her.

"Watch out!" Abigail cried.

The second troll hag tried to pull her hand free, but the two of them tumbled into the water. They screamed once and then sank below the surface.

Hugo and Abigail looked on in horror. Izmerelda stood frozen, and then the troll hag backed away, turned, and flung herself back onto dry land.

The log shifted under their feet as the top of the tree pulled farther away from the bank.

"Jump!" Abigail shouted.

She ran forward, leaping for the bank. Her boots slipped in the mud, but she grabbed at the dried moss that lined the river, and then she was safe on land. She turned, but Hugo stood frozen on the log, the end of which was now buried deep in the water.

"It's too far to jump." He looked over his shoulder. "I'm going back."

"No, there's no time. Just run and jump. I'll catch you."

His eyes met hers. "What if you miss?"

"I won't." She held her hand out. "Trust me."

Water rolled over the top of the log, pushing it farther away.

"Now!" she shouted.

Hugo raced forward and flung himself across the divide. He hit the side of the bank with a *thud*, his feet splashing in the rushing water, which tried to tug him away. Abigail grabbed him under his arms and hauled him to safety.

The trunk washed away, crashing downriver. Izmerelda was left standing alone on the other side, wailing at the loss of her comrades.

"You okay?" Abigail asked

"Yeah." Hugo was pale but nodded firmly. "What now?"

"Now we find Thor."

# Chapter 20

They hiked out of the ravine to a low saddle. A valley spread out before them, scattered boulders pocking the snowy expanse. Buzzards circled lazily overhead. Near a small stand of trees, a large fire burned, sending up a black plume of smoke. Several brawny men stood around it, dressed in thick fur capes and armed with heavy swords that hung at their sides. A few hulking hunting dogs prowled about, sniffing for scraps.

One man in the middle of the group stood out. Golden-haired and broad-shouldered, he was a good head taller than the others. He raised a mug, shouting out something, and his companions roared their approval. Over the fire, a large boar turned on a spit.

"Is that . . ." Abigail couldn't say his name, breathless at the sight of the mighty god.

"Thor," Hugo breathed out, as awestruck as she.

"How can you be sure?"

"Look. His hammer is strapped to his side."

He had his back to them, but when the god turned, flames glinted off the shiny weapon at his waist. Abigail's heart soared. "It's him. He has the hammer."

"And the Belt of Strength, don't forget," Hugo said as the god's cloak parted enough for them to catch the golden sheen. "He's even wearing his gauntlets." The god's hands were encased in a pair of golden gloves.

"So how do we get Thor to hand over his most precious items?"

"By outsmarting him," Hugo said confidently.

"And how do we do that?"

"I've got some ideas. Ready to play along?"

She sighed. "Do I have a choice?"

They started walking down the hill in plain sight. At first, no one noticed them, but as they drew nearer, one of the hounds began barking.

The warriors all turned. Several of them drew their swords, forming a line in front of the fire.

Thor pushed through to see what was happening. His eyes widened in surprise when he saw Abigail and Hugo. "Children, what brings you into the wilds of Jotunheim?"

They stopped in front of him, craning their heads back to see. His golden hair glowed in the afternoon sun. He seemed so big, so powerful, so impossibly *godlike*.

Hugo's tongue was tied. "I-i-it . . ."

Thor squatted down, bringing his face in line with Hugo's. "It?"

"I-it is an honor to meet you," Hugo managed.

Thor winked. "Not every day you meet a god."

"I've met gods before," Abigail said. "I've met Odin. And Vor."

Thor swiveled to look at her. "You've met my father?"

Abigail nodded. "He came to see me once."

"Then you must be special. Tell me, what is your name, child?"

"Abigail. I am . . . that is . . . I am a witch."

Thor frowned. "Why would my father waste time on a witch? He has no fondness for them."

Abigail shrugged. "I suppose because I'm different."

"Different how?"

"Tell him," Hugo urged. "Tell him who your father is."

Abigail hesitated, searching for the right words.

"This sounds like a longer story," Thor said. "Pray, come sit by the fire so that we may be comfortable, and you can tell me everything."

He stood and strode back to the center of the camp. Hugo and Abigail followed, slightly awed by the large figures that stood silently by as the children found a small pile of furs and sank down. Someone passed them a plate of food, and they ate their fill of roasted boar and boiled potatoes.

Thor leaned back on his elbow, a mug of steaming liquid cradled in one hand. "So, children, tell me why I should listen to this story?"

"You knew my father." Abigail set her empty plate to the side. One of the hounds came over and eagerly licked the remains.

Thor stared at her, then laughed loud and long. The others joined in. "Child, you said you were a witchling, did you not? I don't know anyone who consorts with witches."

"Yes, you do," Hugo said. "It was an old friend of yours. His name was Aurvendil."

The entire camp went still. Thor stared at the contents of his mug, swirling it around before he finally spoke in a steely voice. "Do not mention the name of a great warrior in the same breath as a witch, boy, or you will find yourself without your tongue."

"It's true," Abigail said. "Not the Aurvendil you knew, but that story about how you threw his toe into the sky and it became a star? I think part of his spirit continued on. It must have gotten lonely up there, because one day the gods allowed him to come back down to this world, and he met my mother."

"She's lying," one of the warriors said. "Witches have no heart."

"That's right," they all agreed.

"That's what our code dictates," Abigail said. "So there's no reason my mother should have fallen for this Aurvendil, but here I am. I met him, you know."

Thor frowned. "What do you mean?"

"I was there too," Hugo said. "He came down from the heavens when Abigail needed him most and filled her with starshine magic."

"This is preposterous." Thor stood up to kick a log into the fire. "You are full of nonsense. Someone has put you up to this."

Hugo looked at Abigail and then cleared his throat. "The truth is, we've come to warn you."

"Warn me? Do I look as if I need protection?" Thor laughed, and his men joined in.

"We've just come from Utgard-Loki's palace. The king of the giants has been boasting to everyone about how he bested you."

Thor flushed but dismissed Hugo's words with an impatient wave. "An old story. All know it's only because he used trickery and magic to deceive my very senses."

"Yes, but he's issued a new challenge," Hugo said. "To prove to all that he's greater than the mighty Thor, he invites you to his palace for another round of wits, this time without his magic."

Thor pinned Hugo with his stare. "Without his magic I would gladly face him. How do I know it's not another of his tricks?"

"Because he gave up his fjalnar, the charm that contains his magic. He's sitting in his palace on the highest peak across the river, unable to move, just waiting for you to face him."

Thor drew the hammer from his side. "Then I will go beat down his gates with my mighty Mjolnir and show him just what kind of god I am." He hefted the golden hammer in the light of the fire to shouts of approval.

"Er, that's just it," Hugo said. "He's telling everyone you're too scared to face him without your hammer. That your courage comes from Mjolnir and . . . well . . . without it you're nothing but a . . . coward."

"What?" Thor roared with outrage, throwing his hammer across the clearing. It spun through the air, then hit the side of the ravine with a loud crash, causing a small avalanche of snow before flying back into his hand. "No one calls Thor a coward and lives to tell. The giant king will die a slow and painful death at my hands."

Abigail hid a smile. Really, he was so easy to fool. "That's why we came to warn you. You mustn't fall for his tricks. He wants you to show up without your hammer so he can defeat you with his strength. That hammer guarantees your victory. Without it, we all know you would lose."

"Says who?" Thor flushed a deep, angry red. "Am I not a god? Am I such a weakling?" He flexed his biceps, and the men around him roared their approval. "But to travel without my hammer would be foolish."

"That's fine," Abigail said. "We can go back to Utgard-Loki and tell him you won't face him without your hammer. I'm sure he'll understand and let the whole matter drop."

She nodded at Hugo, and they stood, turning to go.

"Stop!" Thor roared. "Do not move, or so help me, I will send this hammer at your heads." The hammer spun in his hand. "I am no coward, but I am suspicious. Why would a loathsome giant like Utgard-Loki send two children to do his bidding? Why should I believe you?"

"You shouldn't," Abigail said, almost hating herself for her lie. "I agreed to come warn you because you knew my father—were a friend to him." She curtsied, hooked arms with Hugo, and began to walk firmly away.

Thor's voice rang out. "So you want nothing?"

Abigail looked over her shoulder and shook her head. "No. Just to warn you. I owed that to my father's memory. Farewell." They continued walking to the tree line.

They'd made it to the edge of the woods when Thor called them back.

"Wait."

Abigail slipped Hugo a grin before they spun about and walked back to the fire. Thor looked troubled, a frown marring his chiseled features.

"It appears I have to face this rival of mine one more time," he said. "I cannot lie, one of the reasons I return to Jotunheim is to find an opportunity to redeem myself. You're certain Utgard-Loki is without his little deceiver?"

"Yes. It is out of his reach," Hugo said firmly. "He cannot use magic to trick you, only his strength."

"I have faced giants before, though none quite as large as the giant king. Honor demands I meet him face to face." Thor tapped the hammer at his side, and his face furrowed in deep thought before clearing. "I will leave my Mjolnir here with you."

"Us?" Hugo said, feigning shock. "You want us to watch it?"

"I have no one else I would trust. My men will insist on accompanying me."

"No, Hugo, we can't," Abigail said. "We did what we came to do. We mustn't linger."

"What do you mean you can't?" Thor said. "Why not?"

"Because we have to go," she said. "Pressing matters call us home."

"What can be more important than guarding the hammer of Thor?" The god put a hand on Abigail's shoulder. "There is no one I would trust more than the daughter of a friend. Surely, for your father, you would do me the honor of guarding my hammer while I go into battle."

Guilt swamped Abigail. Her jaw froze. What was she doing lying to a god like this, in her father's name? "I . . . I suppose, if you insist." The words were chalk in her mouth, but she forced herself to speak them. *For Orkney,* she reminded herself. *To fix all the wrongs that have been done.* "It can't be for very long. Our ship captain awaits us."

"Excellent. It will be no more than three days. We'll leave you with plenty of supplies. You can shelter in the cave just through those trees. There is snow in the air—I can smell it. You will be warm and safe while I rid the world of this giant."

# Chapter 21

"I think they're gone," Hugo said, peering out of the cave Thor had directed them to. "We should get moving."

"It's getting late. Maybe we should stay the night." Abigail avoided his glance. She sat on a smooth stone by the small fire they'd built, staring into the flames.

"It's only just past noon," he said.

"I'm not ready to go yet. And besides, this may be a test to see if we're tricking him. If we leave now, he may catch us stealing away."

Hugo was puzzled, but he shrugged, leaving the entrance to join her by the fire. He sat down on a thick pelt. "Okay, we'll wait a couple hours, but it looks like a storm is moving in." Wind gusted into their cave, causing the flames to flicker and dance.

Hugo must have fallen asleep, because when he awoke, the fire had burned low. Abigail sat in the same position, as if she hadn't moved in hours.

"Why didn't you wake me?" Hugo rubbed the sleep from his eyes and made his way back to the entrance. A thick layer of fresh snow covered the ground, and a sharp wind blew stinging ice crystals into his face. "The storm has set in. We should have left hours ago. Abigail, are you there?" He snapped his fingers in her face, and she raised her head.

"Then we'd be out in that storm." She pointed outside, blinking owlishly. "At least in here we're safe."

"What's wrong? Are you having second thoughts?"

"No. Maybe. I don't know. It just feels so wrong lying to him using my father's name. I feel guilty."

He squatted down and put a hand on her arm. "If we don't take the hammer, then Robert will find a way to take it and use it to destroy your coven."

"And what exactly are we going to do with it?" she said. "The plan was to find someone we could trust to give it to, but . . ."

"They might use it."

"Exactly. There's no one we can trust. Oh, it's all such a mess."

Hugo walked over to the stone shelf that held Thor's precious items. He slipped one of the golden gauntlets onto his hand. It was three sizes too big. The smooth metal was etched with thunderbolts. Setting it down, he ran his fingers over the belt. It was made of woven bands of gold, flexible but strong. He studied the hammer. The hilt was made of a dark wood, smooth to the touch. He gripped it, but even with both hands he couldn't budge Mjolnir.

"Er, Abigail, we might have another problem."

She rose, coming over to stand by him. "What is it?"

"This." He nodded at the hammer. "It's too heavy for me to lift."

She gave it a go, using both hands, and then the two of them tried, but even together they were unable to move it even an inch.

"Well, that's a problem," Abigail said.

A small whimper sounded at the opening to the cave.

Abigail's eyes flew to Hugo's, and a ball of witchfire appeared in her hand. "Did you hear that?"

"Yes. Do you think Izmerelda followed us?"

"Or maybe it's Robert."

"Abigail," a voice called weakly.

She let the witchfire in her hand die. "Safina? Is that you?"

"Abigail," the voice said again. "Help."

"Come on," she said to Hugo. "We have to help her."

"Wait, it could be a trap."

"You think Safina is going to trap me?"

"Not Safina, Endera," he said, but Abigail wasn't listening. She hurried toward the cave entrance, raising a hand to ward off the swirling flakes of snow.

"Safina! Where are you? Show yourself." A small figure huddled in the snow. Abigail hurried over and knelt by the girl's side, rolling her over. "Safina, are you okay?"

Endera looked up at her with eyes full of malice. "Gotcha."

Abigail tried to react, but wiry arms grabbed her from behind, pinning her hands at her sides and preventing her from calling on her witchfire.

"Don't even think about it," Nelly growled in her ear.

Glorian had already wrestled Hugo to the ground and was sitting atop him. Endera got to her feet, shaking the snow off her cloak.

"You know what your problem is, Abigail? You're weak. You care too much for others. It's why I knew you would come running when you heard Safina."

"Where is she? What have you done with her?" Abigail asked, trying to wrestle free.

From behind a tree, Safina appeared, looking defiant. "I'm right here, traitor."

# Chapter 22

ndera stepped into the cave, practically floating with euphoria. After all this time, she had Abigail right where she wanted. Finally, she would get the revenge she deserved and rid the coven once and for all of the vermin known as Abigail Tarkana.

"How did you find us?" Abigail looked spitting mad. She struggled against the strip of cloth Nelly had used to bind her wrists.

"Oh, a little bird told me where you were."

Endera and the others had been walking in circles for hours, searching for any sign of them. The buzzards they had been following had departed with the heavy snowfall. They had crossed a toxic smelling river with the help of a log jammed between rocks, and then become hopelessly lost. Safina had been the one to suggest the divining spell that could trace magic. Endera would have thought of it if the annoying girl hadn't piped up first.

Endera sauntered over to the stone shelf that held Thor's possessions. The golden hammer glowed in the firelight. "I owe you thanks for stealing my prize from Thor."

"It's not yours, and we didn't steal it. He left us with it."

"He left it with you?" Endera burst out laughing. "That's like putting a Shun Kara wolf in charge of a pigeon's nest. You were going to steal it, weren't you? Then give it to those awful Orkadian friends of yours?"

A frown pleated Abigail's brow. "No. Sort of. We planned to borrow it so the Orkadians could have a chance in this war."

Endera shook her head. "Ever the traitor, Abigail. Until your last breath. We will be taking the hammer back to Madame Hestera. One can only imagine what she can do with that kind of power. Oh, and she said I should get rid of you, so I'm afraid you won't be returning to classes."

Abigail paled. "Madame Hestera wouldn't ask such a thing."

"The message from her raven was loud and clear. You and your little friend are not to return. How shall I destroy you?" Endera tapped her chin, pretending to think about it. "Perhaps a choking spell, and I'll watch you turn blue?"

"Hold on," Safina said. "You can't take the word of a raven. Let's just take the hammer and go."

Endera whirled on the girl. "I don't think you understand exactly who is in charge here, and it is not some orphaned firstling. You will do as I ask, or you will be left behind."

"I didn't . . . you wouldn't." Safina blinked wide eyes.

"Watch me."

Safina stumbled back, looking hurt and confused.

"Now, where were we? Oh yes, the choking spell. A little something special my mother taught me. Before you killed her." Endera thrust a hand out, squaring her feet. *"Melera, aspire demora."*

Abigail's hand flew to her throat, and her mouth worked open and closed, but the girl couldn't draw air.

"Endera, this thing weighs a ton," Glorian called.

Endera tore her eyes away from Abigail's suffering. "Must I think of everything?"

She crossed to the stone shelf, shoved Glorian aside, and strapped the Belt of Strength around her waist, then put on the pair of gauntlets. They were far too large, but she used them to grip the hammer handle, and they instantly shrunk to fit her small hands while the belt tightened at her waist. She lifted the hammer easily. "If any of you had paid attention in History of Witchery, you would know you can't handle Mjolnir without the proper tools. Shall we go? I want to be underway before anyone else ventures near."

"What about him?" Nelly pointed at the Balfin boy.

"Leave him. He can see firsthand how a traitor is dealt with by the coven."

She swept past Abigail, ignoring the girl's outstretched hand. What mercy had that traitor shown her mother? None.

Safina made to follow. Endera nodded at Nelly, who shoved the girl back, knocking her to the ground.

"I'm afraid you're of no use to me anymore," she said, then swept on out of the cave.

Outside, the storm had lifted, and the sun was just visible through a break in the clouds. Power coursed through Endera's veins. It was fantastic, really, holding this weapon. She swung the hammer at a large boulder. A shock wave ran up her arm, knocking her back teeth together, but the heavy boulder rolled sideways as if it weighed as much as a pebble, sealing the entrance to the cave.

Endera waited for satisfaction to fill her. She had done it. Bested her nemesis. Proven she was the superior witch. "This is for you, mother," she whispered, but not even that thought sent a spark of joy through her.

# Chapter 23

*T*his is bad. *So bad.* Hugo wrestled with the binds that held his wrists. Abigail was turning blue, her eyes searching his desperately. *Do something,* she mouthed at him.

Safina sat staring at the dwindling fire, her eyes round with shock.

"Safina, untie me! We have to help Abigail."

"Don't speak to me," she said woodenly.

"Abigail is going to die if we don't do something. Please." He tugged harder at his binds, chafing his wrists raw, but Nelly had tied them too tight.

"Abigail is a traitor to the coven."

"No, she's trying to make things better. You know this war is going to end badly."

The girl shrugged her thin shoulders. "So? The witches will win."

"Yes, but at what price? If all of Orkney falls, the gods will come down and erase it as if it never was."

She frowned. "They wouldn't dare."

"They would. You're smart, Safina. Endera is set on punishing Abigail for what happened to her mother, but you were there that night. You know it wasn't Abigail's fault."

Safina absorbed his words, then said, "Why do you care so much for a witchling who intended to betray you?"

"What do you mean?"

"The raven that's following Abigail—she's been reporting back to Madame Hestera. She was to get rid of you. That's what Madame Hestera ordered."

Shock flooded Hugo. Emenor's words came back to him. *The witches will double-cross you every time.* He couldn't speak. He looked over at Abigail. Her eyes had fluttered closed, and she slumped sideways onto the furs.

Safina frowned. "Wait, you didn't know that Abigail was reporting your every move to the ravens?"

"No, but it doesn't matter. She had her reasons."

"Yes, it does." The witchling looked excited. "She's betraying you, which means maybe I've misunderstood her all along."

Hugo couldn't stop the sharp stab of pain. "So now you're willing to help?"

"Now I have hope that Abigail is a true witch," Safina said with a grin. "First things first, we have to bring her around so she can help us get out of here."

They turned Abigail onto her back. The girl was white as chalk, and her chest didn't rise at all. *Were they too late?*

"We learned a spell this week in Spectacular Spells to shock someone. Maybe it will snap her out of it." Safina wriggled her fingers. "*Elisay, chaka tora.*" She shot a thin stream of witchfire at Abigail's chest.

The girl jolted but didn't breathe.

"Do it again," Hugo said.

"*Elisay, chaka tora.*" Safina sent another bolt. Once more, Abigail jolted but still didn't breathe.

"It's not working," Safina said. "We left it too long."

"No. Do it again—use more witchfire this time."

Safina clenched her fingers tightly, then shouted the words. "*Elisay, chaka tora!*" This time she shot a large stream of witchfire. Abigail jolted and bucked, then suddenly sat up, gasping in a deep breath.

"What happened?" She looked at them, her eyes wide with shock.

"Safina saved you," Hugo said.

"Thank you." Abigail turned grateful eyes on the young witchling.

Safina gripped her hand. "Abigail, I'm sorry I've been such a toad. I didn't realize what a true witch you were all this time. I should have never listened to Endera."

Abigail frowned. "What do you mean a true witch?"

"You've been spying on Hugo, reporting back to Madame Hestera. Bristle told us everything. If you'd betray your best friend for your coven, that proves your loyalty."

"I wasn't—" she protested, but Hugo cut her off.

"It's fine, Abigail, a witch is a witch." He gave her a look that warned her not to argue.

Her eyes went to the empty stone shelf. "Endera took the hammer—but how did she manage to lift it?"

"She put on the belt and gauntlets, which I should have figured out for myself," Hugo said. "She walked right out with it."

"We have to go after her." Abigail tried to stand, but her knees wavered.

Hugo gripped her elbow, steadying her. "Just one problem—she's trapped us in here with a boulder in front of the entrance. If I had some magic, I might be able to make an opening."

Abigail held her palm out. Her hand shook, but she managed a small ball of witchfire. Hugo dangled his medallion over the flames, replenishing its magic, and then waved it in front of the rock, chanting, *"Fein kinter, terminus."*

The rock swirled, but no opening appeared. He tried again, repeating the words louder, but the rock swirl died and wouldn't return.

"Why isn't it working?" he asked.

"Endera probably cast a protection spell on it," Abigail said. "Maybe if all three of us push on it."

They tried pushing with all their strength, but the rock didn't budge.

"Again," Abigail said.

They put their shoulders into it, and suddenly, the rock rolled away, letting in daylight.

Hugo and the two witchlings staggered out into a crowd of dwarfs pointing swords at them. In the center stood a tall boy with brown hair.

"Give us the hammer of Thor or face execution," Robert said.

# Chapter 24

"**W**e don't have it," Abigail said, fighting back the lingering headache that made talking painful. "Endera took it, along with his Belt of Strength and gauntlets."

Robert flushed angrily. "You lie. It's here. Search the cave," he ordered.

Obie and Mullet moved past them and emerged a few moments later.

"No sign of it," Obie said.

Robert raised the point of his sword until it touched Abigail's throat. Around his neck, he wore the leather pouch his father had given him the night Vertulious returned. It held a shard of Odin's Stone, a remnant of a once great power. "Tell me where she took it, or so help me, on Odin's breath, I will end your life this moment."

Abigail stared back at him and then raised her hand, pushing the tip of the sword away. "No, you won't. We were friends. I'm still your friend."

His eyes clouded with hurt. "You turned your back on me when I needed you the most."

"No, when you needed me the most, I was there time

and again. Or have you forgotten who tried to help you find Odin's Stone? Who tried to save your life that night? Who did everything in their power to help fix a problem you created? The only thing I failed you in was not turning my back on my coven. If I had stepped forward, they would have kicked me out, and Hugo's family would have been turned into the street. Is that what you wanted?"

"No." He slowly sheathed his sword. "I guess I didn't look at it that way."

"We are your friends," Hugo said. "We came here to get Thor's hammer to stop the war."

"You would have turned it over to my father?" Robert asked. "To destroy the very thing you claim to love?"

"No." Abigail bit her lip. "We don't want you to use it against us, we just want the coven to think that you would. To even the sides and stop them from going to war."

Robert frowned. "You think that will work? Vertulious seems keen on ruling over Orkney, no matter the cost."

"It can work," Hugo said. "First we have to stop Endera from taking the hammer back to Madame Hestera. Odin only knows what she'll do with it."

"Hugo's right," Abigail said. "And if Vertulious gets his hands on it, this war will be over before it's begun. There will be nothing left but ashes and dust."

Rego looked at Robert. "They make sense, lad."

Robert hesitated, then nodded. "Which way would she have gone?"

Hugo and Abigail turned to Safina, who looked uncertain.

"Please, Safina, we need to stop them." Abigail put a hand on the witchling's arm.

Safina sighed. "Madame Hestera has a boat waiting due west of here."

"Then that's the direction we go," Rego said.

After that, it was easy enough to pick up Endera's trail. The three girls' tracks followed a winding path through the woods. They set a brisk pace—Abigail felt an urgency in her bones. If Endera made it onto the ship, everything they'd worked for would be lost.

"How far is it to the sea?" Abigail asked between ragged puffs.

Rego answered without slowing. "Two hours, maybe less."

"Do you think we can catch them?" she asked.

"We can try."

Rego picked up the pace. Abigail's lungs burned, but she didn't dare stop and catch her breath. She doggedly followed in Rego's steps, with Hugo, Robert, and the others right behind her.

When she was sure she couldn't run another step, the trees thinned, and she caught a glimpse of pale sunlight glinting off the sea. Waves crashed against barnacle-crusted rocks, sending up flying spray. They burst out of the woods to find Endera and her two cronies standing amid scattered piles of seaweed and driftwood. A large raven was perched on a rock in front of Endera.

At their arrival, Endera held up Thor's hammer. "Don't come any closer. I'm taking this back to Madame Hestera, and together we are going to rid the coven of that he-witch, and then the war can really begin."

"Yes," the raven cawed. "Madame Hestera awaits her prize. Sadly, she is going to be disappointed."

A shiver ran up Abigail's spine. It couldn't be . . . but that oily rasp was unmistakable. "Endera, that's not Hestera's raven."

"Of course it is," Endera snapped. She turned back to the raven. "Bristle, what do you mean, disappointed? I have what she asked. Where is the ship she promised?"

"The ship has sunk," the bird rasped back.

"Sunk?"

The raven flared its wings. "Give me the hammer, and I will take it to her."

Endera laughed. "You? You're nothing but a feathered bag of bones. I'm not giving her pet the most powerful weapon in this world."

"I think you will," it said.

The raven's body puffed out into a round ball and grew in size, doubling and then tripling. Feathers flew in the air as it shook. Its wings shifted and turned into arms. Splayed talons turned into booted feet. The black head morphed and grew and shimmied until, with a loud pop, Vertulious appeared, wearing his familiar blue robes.

"You," Endera whispered.

"Me." He spread his arms. "Ah, it gets tiresome being cramped in such a small body. I missed my arms and legs."

Endera raised her hand to throw the hammer, but Vertulious snapped his fingers, and she froze, captured in his spell.

"Tsk, tsk, plotting behind my back. I will have words with Madame Hestera next I see her." He undid the belt at her waist, and the heavy hammer dropped to the sand. The gauntlets slipped off her hands. The old alchemist lifted the items and strapped them on.

Behind Vertulious, the red-eyed shreek-Omera landed in the sand, snarling and baring vicious teeth.

Vertulious turned to Abigail. "Come with me. This war will be our shared victory."

"I'll never follow you," Abigail snapped.

"Pity. You know who you are, do you not?"

"I know exactly who I am. Abigail Tarkana. Witch. Loyal member to my coven. But also loyal to this world."

He shook his head. "You sell yourself short. There can be only one Curse Breaker, and while I like to pretend it is me, there is no mystery as to who the real Curse Breaker is."

"What do you mean?" Abigail's heart thudded in her chest.

"You know it is you. Deny it all you want. It remains true."

"The prophecy wasn't even real," she said. "Rubicus just made that up after he met me."

"No. The prophecy was a promise he made to Odin before he met you. Call it a time warp paradox—in the first version he hadn't met you, but he swore someone would come along and break Odin's curse. Then when he met you, he knew it would happen. He was just wrong about how. Right the first time."

"You're lying."

"I lie about many things, but not this. I traced your bloodline, you know. The Tarkanas were a weaker offshoot of the Volgrim witches, but your bloodline traces back directly to Rubicus himself." He swung a leg over the back of the Omera. "Last chance to join with me."

"I'm going to destroy you."

Vertulious laughed and reached into the pocket of his robe to pull out a shiny red apple. He bit into the flesh, savoring the bite. "Not as long as I have a collection of these delicious apples, my dear."

Shock rooted Abigail in place. "But you can't . . . there was only one."

"One is all it takes if you are crafty and harvest the seeds."

"You planted a tree," she said in disbelief.

His smile mocked her. "I will live for eternity, while you will die here along with your friends." He cast his hand out over the sand, murmuring indistinct words before the shreek-Omera launched into flight.

Hugo came to Abigail's side. "Die with your friends? What did he mean by that?"

"Um, I think he meant those." Robert drew his sword as several green serpents burst through the sand, rearing their heads up and hissing.

# Chapter 25

"What are they?" Abigail jumped back, sending a small streak of witchfire at the closest one.

"Sand snakes. Very poisonous." Rego swung his sword at a pair, neatly removing their heads. "One bite and you're a goner. We need to get off the sand and back into the trees."

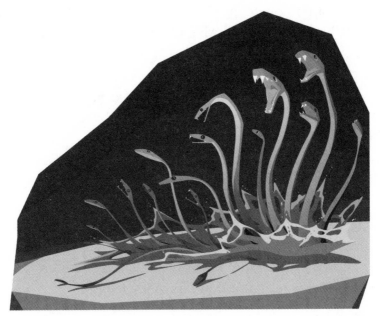

"You! This is all your fault!" Endera launched herself at Abigail, catching her by surprise and knocking her back onto the sand. "You killed my mother," she screamed, wrapping her hands around Abigail's throat. "You ruined everything!"

Abigail clawed at Endera's hands, but she couldn't unlock the girl's grip. Stars danced behind her eyelids. And then something shoved Endera off her.

She gasped in air, shocked to see the stocky figure of Glorian over her. "We have bigger problems, Endera. We need Abigail's help."

Endera snarled, getting to her feet and calling up a ball of witchfire, but a snake burst out of the sand in front of her, and she quickly threw the witchfire at it instead, incinerating it.

Around them, more and more snakes popped out of the sand, forcing their group to take refuge on a small pile of rocks. The witchlings threw blasts of witchfire while the dwarfs and Robert hacked at the snakes with their swords, but no matter how many they struck down, more appeared.

"What do we do?" Abigail said, panting. "We can't hold them off forever."

"Ahoy!" a voice called. "Need a ride?"

"Jasper!" Abigail had never been so happy to see his ragged ship at anchor. The old sailor bobbed in the sea a few yards from shore in a small rowboat.

"I can't take you all at once," he warned.

"I'm going first." Endera shoved her way forward. She sprayed witchfire across the sand, driving the serpents back, and then raced toward the water with Nelly and Glorian at her heels.

"Hugo, go. Don't be brave," Abigail added as he started to argue. "You don't have a weapon."

Hugo gave in and raced after the others, dodging snakes that popped up at his feet.

"You too," Rego said to Abigail, but she refused.

"No. My witchfire will hold them off."

"I'll help." Safina took a fighting stance on a rock at Abigail's side.

Rego nodded at Mullet and Obie. The pair hobbled across the sand, hacking at the snakes that snapped at their ankles.

Jasper began rowing the boat back to his ship, leaving them alone on the beach.

The snakes crowded closer, slithering over the tops of the rocks, more and more appearing with every passing second.

"There are too many of them." Robert gasped with exertion as he kept hacking. "They just keep multiplying."

Abigail's arms trembled with fatigue. She didn't have much magic left in her. What was going to happen when she ran out of witchfire?

Jasper had started rowing back to shore, but the space between the rocks and the waterline was a solid green mass of squirming, slithering snakes.

As her witchfire sputtered out, Abigail dropped her arms, exhausted. Safina did the same. They started kicking at the snakes. One bit down on the toe of Abigail's boot, but Robert was there to hack its head off.

Abigail shook her head. "We'll never make it to the water."

"I'll clear a path," Rego said.

"No, that's a death wish. You'll be bitten for sure."

A streak of fur bolted across the sand, attacking a snake and wrestling it to the ground. It was a hoblet with a white spot on its forehead. Another one joined it, then another, until more than a dozen of them darted and danced among the snakes, driving a wedge in the reptiles. They struck fast, tossing the snakes aside with their sharp teeth.

"Run!" Jasper shouted.

Abigail didn't hesitate. She raced across the strip of sand between the line of hoblets, followed closely by Safina, Robert, and Rego. They splashed into the water and flung themselves onto the boat, heaving a sigh of relief as Jasper rowed them away.

On shore, the sand snakes were slithering back into their holes as the hoblets continued to give chase. One of the hoblets—the one with the white spot on its forehead—rose up on its back paws. It looked directly at Abigail, bobbing its head once. It looked just like the one she had rescued from Izmerelda in the forest.

"Thank you," she whispered, waving goodbye.

It was crowded on board the little ship. The dwarfs went below. Safina went with them, too exhausted to stand. Endera moved to the front of the boat, standing stiffly with her back to them. Nelly hung at her side, looking shaken.

Glorian huddled in the back, shivering.

"Here." Abigail put a blanket around her shoulders. "Thanks for your help."

"I didn't mean . . . I don't like you . . . I mean, I don't *not* like you," the girl mumbled. "It's just, someone had to stop her. She's gone mad with this revenge."

"Agreed," Abigail said. "So again, thanks for your help."

Hugo stood with Robert and Jasper at the helm.

"There's no time to waste," Robert said. "If we don't get to Garamond and stop Vertulious, the war will be over."

"Can you get us there before Vertulious?" Abigail asked. "He left on an Omera."

"Even a son of Aegir can't call up a wind that fast," Jasper said with a scowl. "We might find help elsewhere,

though it's a bargain with the devil," he muttered. The sailor disappeared below deck and reappeared with a large conch horn. He put it to his lips and blew loud and long.

It took a moment, but a gust of wind raced across the sea. Ripples broke the surface, and there was a flash of a silver tail. Then, beside the ship, a red-haired woman appeared.

Amarina.

"Why does the Son of Aegir call on us?" she asked, bobbing next to the ship.

"We need your help," Abigail said. "We have to get to Garamond to stop Vertulious."

The mermaid's eyes were like liquid silver as she gazed at Jasper. "You will owe the queen of the seas a favor, Son of Aegir. Do you agree?"

Abigail looked at Jasper. His jaw locked tight, but he gave a stiff nod.

"Say it," the mermaid said.

"I agree," he bit out, then turned and stalked back to his helm.

With a flip of her tail, the mermaid disappeared from sight. The sea ruffled, and then the ship jumped forward as the mermaids began pulling it through the water. In moments, they were racing across the sea.

"Do you think we'll arrive in time?" Robert gripped the railing as the wind whipped at his hair.

Abigail slipped her arm in his. "Yes. I'm just not sure what we're going to do when we get there."

Hugo stepped up on Robert's other side. "We have to stop him. Once and for all."

"Any ideas?" Abigail asked.

Hugo looked grim. "Not yet. But I'm working on it."

# Chapter 26

awn was breaking when Abigail roused herself, stretching her stiff muscles. She had fallen asleep on the deck of the ship, leaning against the hull. Robert and Hugo were asleep next to her. Steep cliffs rose in front of them. A stone fortress sat proudly overlooking the sea, its red flags snapping in the stiff breeze. She nudged the boys awake.

"Skara Brae!" Robert scrambled up. "I'm home."

"Not quite," Hugo said as Jasper's ship nosed around a point, and the harbor came into view. Black-sailed warships lined the shore, more than a dozen in all. "They've set up a blockade."

Waves of Balfin soldiers were unloading from rowboats and lining the beach. Witches moved among them. Winged creatures dotted the sky. *Omeras*. On the back of each were two witches.

"Do you see Vertulious?" Abigail asked, scanning the skies.

"Not yet."

"So what's the plan?" Robert asked.

"Stop him from using the hammer," Hugo said.

"How?"

"I'm working on it. Jasper, can you get us to shore?"

"That's a mighty unfriendly greeting party waiting. You'll have to take the rowboat around the point and find a less crowded place to land."

A sudden splash sounded. They ran to the other side of the ship. Endera and Nelly were rowing away in the small rowboat, a shamefaced Glorian with them.

"Come back!" Abigail shouted. "We need that boat."

But Endera rowed on, heading straight for the Balfin army on shore.

"I have to get to my father now and warn him to evacuate the city," Robert said. "If Vertulious uses Thor's hammer, the entire city will be destroyed."

"Back in the day, I may have smuggled a thing or two in and out of the city," Jasper said. "If they've not closed it off, there's an underground tunnel that leads inside the walls. You'll have to swim for it and find the entrance."

"We can help," Amarina said from the water. She had surfaced without them noticing. "We will take you there." Around her, other mermaids bobbed.

"I'm coming with you," Abigail said.

"And me," Hugo added.

"Don't think I'm missing out on this," Safina said bravely, popping up from the deck below.

"And us," Rego added from behind her. He looked a little green around the gills. "Can't take another minute on this ship."

Robert tucked his leather pouch inside his shirt, undid his sword and held it in one hand, then took his boots off and held them in the other. Abigail slipped off her boots, and Hugo did the same.

"Ready?" Robert said.

They nodded and, on the count of three, jumped into the water.

The cold hit Abigail hard, taking her breath away. Her mouth filled with seawater. She flailed her arms, holding on to her boots, as her head surfaced. Another wave rolled toward her, and this time she held her breath, waited for it to pass, and floated back up. And then Amarina was there, hooking one arm around her and swimming forward with powerful thrusts of her tail.

They struck out for the cliffs. Abigail snatched breaths when she could—the sea was relentless, constantly forcing them under.

"Where is the entrance?" Hugo shouted, turning every which way in the water. They were close to the cliffs. Jagged rocks protruded into the sea. A large wave would smash them up against them, even with the help of the mermaids.

"I think I see it. This way." Robert ducked under the surface, and they followed, kicking hard as the current swept them close to the cliffs. A black hole appeared in the cliff face. It was nestled behind an outcrop of rock and impossible to see unless you were right up on it.

Amarina released her, and Abigail was swept forward into the channel. She pushed off against the side and drifted. Once she felt rocks under her feet, she stumbled forward, coughing out seawater. Rego pulled her up onto a rock.

They were in a low cave. A rusty iron ring set in the wall was the only indication anyone had been there before. Everyone put on their boots and began climbing over the rocks to a sandy trail. They followed it upward until they reached a heavy steel door.

Robert pushed on it, but the door was locked from the other side. "Now what?"

"Now I get us out of here." Hugo took out his medallion and recited a spell. A small opening appeared, and he snicked his hand through, sliding back the bolt before the opening sealed up.

The door opened on rusty hinges. A set of steps hewn out of solid rock led upward. Robert raced up them two at a time and threw open the door at the top, tumbling into a room.

A group of men and women in official robes were assembled around a large table. They turned, shocked to see the bedraggled group.

"Father!"

Lord Barconian strode over and gripped Robert by the shoulders. "Robert, are you okay? Where have you been?" He pulled the boy into a tight hug and looked over his shoulder at Rego. "Took you long enough to find him."

"You're welcome." Rego bowed slightly. "The boy is more trouble than you know."

Robert pulled free. "I have terrible news, Father. I went after Thor's hammer, only I failed. And now Vertulious has it."

The room filled with gasps. A slender man in shimmering green robes strode over. "What did you say?" He was young, no more than twenty, with oversized eyes that were a deep aquamarine. Most strikingly, his long hair was alabaster white.

*An Eifalian*, Abigail thought, one of the other races on Orkney.

"Gael, he is only a boy," Lord Barconian cautioned.

"A boy who may have cost us the entire war," the Eifalian snapped.

Another even stranger-looking man approached. This one had a hawklike beak for a nose and long black hair tied back in a braid. Feathers dangled from his earlobes.

A *Falcory*. Abigail had read about them, of course, but never seen one in person.

"The hammer of Thor? Why would a god give his mighty Mjolnir to an evil creature like Vertulious?" the hawk-faced man asked, his eyes like flint.

"Actually, he gave it to me." Abigail stepped forward. "I was hoping to use it to stop the war."

Gael sniffed at her. "I smell magic on you. And you," he said of Safina. "These are witchlings." He glared at Robert. "You brought witches into our High Council?"

"They're not like the other witches," Robert said.

"Isn't this the one who betrayed you that night?" Lord Barconian nodded at Abigail.

"Yes, but it wasn't her fault," Robert added quickly. "They would have kicked her out of her coven, and Hugo's family would have been turned into the streets. They didn't have a choice."

"When choice mattered, look at who they chose," his father reminded him. "We cannot allow them to be here."

"We're not leaving until we fix things," Abigail said. "Vertulious will be here any minute, and he won't stop until this city is in ruins."

"Don't you see, Father? You must evacuate the city," Robert said. "We can't beat him."

"We can't run from this," his father said, the lines etched deep into his face. "We must face it and find a way to defeat him. Rego, take them to the catacombs with the other women and children. They'll be safe enough there."

"No! I want to help. I can fight." Robert put a hand on his sword.

His father shook his head wearily. "You are not ready for this kind of battle. Go now and let us resume our planning." He turned to the Eifalian. "Gael, are your archers in place?"

The council resumed their war planning as Rego shoved the children out of the room. Out in the hallway, their small group clustered into a knot.

"I'm not going to the catacombs," Robert said to Rego, "so don't think you can make me."

"Or me," Abigail said.

"Or me," Hugo added.

"I'm with them," Safina piped in.

Rego scratched at his whiskers. "I figure there's not a chance of us winning today, unless one of you has a plan?"

"I can beat him," Abigail said. "I'm the only one with magic strong enough to do it."

"Abigail, he'll destroy you," Hugo said.

"No. Remember, I've seen the inside of his spellbook. It's like seeing inside his head. I have to face him, and then I'll find a way to beat him at his own game."

The normally gruff Obie grunted. "You're not like any witch I ever met."

"When have you ever met a witch?" Mullet asked.

"Never. But she's a good one, I can tell."

A loud horn sounded from the sea.

"That's a Balfin war horn," Hugo said.

"Then Vertulious has arrived," Abigail said calmly. "We should greet him properly."

Rego led them out a side entrance. The cobblestoned streets were deserted. Row after row of Orkadian guards dressed in red uniforms filled the ramparts, waiting for the battle to begin. Several battalions stood in formation behind the large gates, ready to be sent out to fight. *Maybe even to die*, Abigail thought with a shudder.

Rego led them through the streets to a smaller less-used rear gate. The guard argued with Rego, but Robert ordered him to open it under his father's orders. The reluctant guard cracked the gate open just enough to let them out, then slammed it shut behind them.

As if a gate would stop what was coming.

They followed a narrow trail down to the shore, arriving just as the shreek-Omera carrying Vertulious landed with a loud *thump*.

The odious he-witch sprang down and strode over to them. "Abigail, how delightful! You've decided to join me after all."

Before Abigail could tell him what she thought, a group of witches led by Hestera approached. They were mostly older, members of the High Witch Council, and aligned with Hestera. The younger up-and-coming witches were more enthralled with the promises of power Vertulious made.

The old witch shook her cane at him. "Now, see here, Vertulious, the hammer of Thor is too much power for one witch. I demand you hand it over."

"So you can use it against me the way you plotted?"

Her eyes narrowed. "I am still the leader of this coven."

"Are you?" An enormous ball of witchfire appeared in Vertulious's hand. The other witches drew back, leaving Hestera alone to face him. He rolled the witchfire over his palm. "You think yourself more powerful than I? You're nothing but a dried-up hag whose powers have long faded. I should have rid this coven of you when I returned."

He flicked his wrist, and the witchfire zinged toward her so fast it was a blur.

Hestera twirled her emerald cane in front of her, and the witchfire snuffed out with a loud *pop*.

"I still have a few tricks," she sneered. "It's past time someone put you in your place."

She thrust her cane out to the side. Swords rattled in the scabbards of the waiting Balfin soldiers. Hestera swung the cane forward, pointing the emerald tip at the alchemist, and the swords magically unsheathed. The weapons flew through the air, aimed directly at Vertulious's chest.

He clasped his hands over his head, and the swords froze in midair. Then he threw his hands forward, and the swords turned, arrowing back at Hestera. She waved her cane through the air, but the swords kept coming.

Abigail acted quickly. "*Escudio!*" She thrust both hands forward. A bubble of energy sprang up around the old witch, and the swords clanked harmlessly to the ground.

But Vertulious didn't stop. He spit witchfire at Hestera, bursting the bubble, and continued blasting. The old witch dodged over and over, evading his blasts until she was pushed up against the rocks, cowering back from him. He let the witchfire die.

"Your time is up, you dried-up bag of bones. It is I who rule this coven now." He put his fingers to his lips and gave a loud, piercing whistle.

Around him, witches descended from the sky, landing their Omeras with loud *thumps*. Abigail almost cried out with joy when she recognized Big Mama. But the normally fierce Omera's eyes were dull, and her head hung low. All the other Omeras wore similar expressions, with the exception of the shreek-Omera. It was horrible to see the magnificent creatures enslaved.

Vertulious held up Thor's hammer. "In my hands I hold the most powerful weapon this world has ever seen. With my powers and this hammer, we can destroy the hold the Orkadians have over us and claim this world as ours."

"No," Abigail said. "If you use that hammer, if you threaten the balance in this world, the gods will erase this place."

"The gods sit on their high thrones looking down their

noses at us. Judging us," Vertulious argued. "Once we take control, they will have no choice but to bargain with us."

"The way Odin bargained with Rubicus," a witch shouted. "He cut his head off."

A sliver of hope ran through Abigail. Someone had stood up for them. Other witches grumbled.

"Rubicus was a fool," Vertulious said. "I hold the power of the universe in my hands." He raised the hammer and then threw it across the water at a distant outcrop. There was a loud rumble, and the bluff disintegrated, crumbling into the sea.

The hammer spun back to his hand. "I have the power to rip through any fortress. Destroy any stronghold. Wipe out entire armies. I can even destroy the wall that protects Asgard. The gods think they can erase this place, but if they dare set foot on these lands, it is I who will erase them. Who stands with me?"

The beach was silent. Abigail crossed her fingers, hoping the witches would stand against him, but a Balfin soldier hurried forward. His black uniform had ornate gold trim on the shoulders. A boy scrambled after him, holding the man's sword and helmet in his arms. The boy was shaking so badly he dropped the helmet in the sand and bent to pick it up.

"Oskar? Is that you?" Hugo asked.

The boy looked up at Hugo, and hatred filled his eyes. "Coward, you ran away, and I had to take your place."

"Lieutenant DeGroot, at your service." The soldier bowed to Vertulious. "The Black Guard stands ready to destroy our enemy."

DeGroot took his sword from Oskar and lofted it into the air. The Balfin army responded with a thumping of their boots and a rallying cry. Several of the young witch acolytes released high-pitched screeches, washing the entire beach in thrumming noise.

Smugly triumphant, Vertulious held up a hand for quiet. "Let them feel our wrath before I wipe them out of existence."

He crossed his arms, signaling the ships. Witches were positioned with Balfin soldiers on each one. They placed giant balls of witchfire onto mounted catapults and launched them into the sky.

The fireballs flew in an arc and landed inside the city walls. Spires of smoke began to rise. One after the other, witches took to the air on the backs of Omeras, circling in the sky, ready to rain more witchfire down.

A volley of arrows sped out from the Orkadian stronghold, but Vertulious waved his arm, sending a ceiling of protection over the entire beach. The arrows fell harmlessly to the ground.

"And now we advance." He looked down at Abigail. "I should eliminate you and your little friends for interfering, but I'd rather you lived to watch everything you care about be destroyed."

He climbed aboard his shreek-Omera and left them on the beach.

# Chapter 27

Abigail rushed to Madame Hestera's side. The old witch rested against a rock. "Are you all right?" she asked, putting a hand on her shoulder.

The old witch threw her hand off. "This is all your doing, witchling. Fix it, or don't bother returning to the Tarkana coven."

Stunned, Abigail got to her feet. Someone shoved her to the side.

"Move it," Endera said. "You've done enough damage." She knelt by Madame Hestera, putting an arm around her shoulders.

Abigail woodenly rejoined the others.

"What do we do now?" Hugo asked.

"We have to go after him," Robert said. "If he breaches the wall, Skara Brae will be lost."

"I'm afraid nothing can stop a witch that powerful, not with a weapon like that," Rego said. "I think it best we get you somewhere safe."

"No, I'm not leaving my father," Robert said.

"If only we had something to fight back with," Abigail said. "A weapon of our own."

"Um, Abigail, what's that?" Hugo pointed at the sea.

Something swelled under the surface. The Balfin warships swayed and tossed. The soldiers ran to the side of the ships, looking overboard.

"Is it the mermaids?" Robert asked.

"No. Look." Abigail almost laughed out loud as a mass of cinnamon hair appeared, then a forehead, then a nose.

A familiar giant rose out of the water. He swatted at one of the ships, sending the men inside tumbling into the sea.

Utgard-Loki waded onto the shore.

"Where is my fjalnar?" the giant king roared. Behind him, four more giants appeared, sending waves crashing onto the docks as they walked out of the water.

"Utgard-Loki, it's me." Abigail waved her arms. "We need your help."

He lowered himself down to her level, scowling. "You sent Thor after me."

"Without his hammer," she reminded him. "Just like I promised. Did you beat him again?"

"No. It was a draw. He was strong, but he couldn't best me. Now, where is the thief with my fjalnar?"

"I have it." Robert lifted his tunic. Underneath, a leather cord strung with several yellowed teeth was wound several times around his waist. He untied it and handed it over to the giant. "We need your help. There's a powerful he-witch—he stole Thor's hammer. He's going to destroy my city."

Utgard-Loki strung the cord around his wrist, sighing with relief once it was tied. "Giants don't fight for humans."

"Do they fight for this world?" Hugo said. "Because if we don't stop this, bad things are going to happen to us all."

"Please," Abigail added. "What if he decides to go after Jotunheim next? You won't be able to hide forever."

Utgard-Loki sighed and then plucked Abigail up between two fingers and put her on his shoulder. Two other giants picked up Robert and Hugo.

"What about me?" Safina said. "I want to fight."

"Stay with Madame Hestera and the others," Abigail called down. "She is the leader of our coven, and nothing must happen to her."

Safina nodded.

"I think we'll walk," Rego said, keeping a safe distance from the giants.

Hugo called out from his perch atop the giant's shoulder, "Oskar, you're not afraid of a giant, are you?"

The boy covered his head with his hands, clearly trying to be invisible as he huddled behind a rock.

The giants lumbered up the road in long strides until the battlefield came into view. A curtain of black smoke rose from inside the city. The Balfin army had formed lines in front of the thick walls of the fortress. Witches circled overhead on their Omeras, waiting for the signal to send down blasts of witchfire.

A battalion of Orkadian soldiers were lined up outside the gates, prepared to do battle. Abigail thought she recognized Robert's father on horseback out front, encouraging his men. Falcory warriors mixed among them, and rows of Eifalian archers lined the parapets, their white hair and colorful robes making them stand out.

Vertulious stood in front of the Orkadian battalion, unafraid, hammer in hand. The pompous he-witch was clearly enjoying drawing out the moment of the Orkadians' demise. At the lumbering sound of their approach, he turned, and his jaw dropped in shock.

The giants began swatting this way and that with their meaty hands, sending entire divisions hurling through the air. Several of the Balfins stabbed at the giants' feet with their swords, but it just annoyed the giants. They kicked at the soldiers and sent even more of them flying. The giants cut a swath through the army as they stomped their way forward, scattering unit after unit.

"My beautiful army!" Vertulious cried. He raised the hammer and threw it at Utgard-Loki. There was a gust of wind and a distant booming sound, and then the hammer returned to Vertulious's hand.

"Hmm . . ." Utgard-Loki scratched his chin. "It felt as though a pebble was thrown at me."

Vertulious gasped. "That's impossible. I threw the hammer straight at your head. I must have missed." He raised his arm and threw the hammer again, aiming directly at Utgard-Loki's nose.

Again there was a rush of air and a distant rumble, and then the hammer was back in the hand of Vertulious.

Utgard-Loki yawned. "Is it always this dusty here on Garamond? I swear there are pebbles falling from the sky."

"How are you still standing?" Vertulious said. "Impossible!" Rage twisted his features, and he threw the hammer with both hands. This time the giant caught it in midair and used it to scratch his nose.

"Ah, that's better," he said. "I had an itchy."

Vertulious raised his hand to call the hammer back, but it didn't budge. Abigail looked down at Utgard-Loki's fist and almost laughed out loud when she realized he had wrapped his fjalnar around the shaft.

Vertulious held his hand out, shaking it in the air, but the hammer still didn't move. "Give me back my hammer!" he shrieked.

"Put me down," Abigail said in the giant's ear. "And whatever you do, don't let go of Mjolnir." Utgard-Loki lifted her and set her down in front of Vertulious.

"It's time you and I settled this," Abigail said.

Impatience flared across his features. "I grow tired of your interference." He crossed Thor's gauntlets together. Sparks flashed and a thunderbolt erupted, sending jagged lightning at her, followed by a boom so loud it hurt her eardrums. She had no time to throw up a protection spell. Instead she dove to the side as the powerful force sent her tumbling in the dirt. Hugo and Robert helped her to her feet.

"How can we help?" Robert asked.

"Stay out of this," she said. "He belongs to me."

"You think you can best me, little witch?" Vertulious sneered. "I would enjoy showing you all the ways I can make you feel pain, but I have a war to finish."

"How can you without your hammer?" Abigail challenged.

"Do you forget I am a powerful he-witch? You think I can't turn this fortress into rubble with a mere spell?" He turned as the shreek-Omera landed next to him and smoothly leaped onto its back, casting her a taunting look before taking flight.

Abigail whistled, hoping Big Mama would still come, but it was a smaller Omera that landed next to her. "Starfire! But how . . ."

The young Omera must have followed the others, but his eyes were bright and clear—they hadn't bothered enchanting him. Abigail didn't hesitate—she leaped on his back and gave chase.

Vertulious banked over the stone walls of the fortress, motioning with his hand as he cast his spell. Stones tumbled from the corner rampart towers, sending soldiers flying through the air. He was dismantling the fortress walls stone by stone. She had to find a way to draw him away, and fast.

Abigail blasted witchfire at his shreek-Omera. It staggered but kept going. Starfire was sleek and fast, quickly gaining on the other beast. Abigail blasted again. This time Vertulious wheeled around and headed straight for her.

The he-witch raised his hand, using Thor's gauntlets to send ear-splitting thunderbolts at her. She turned Starfire on his side, veering left and out over the water.

"Come on, follow me," she whispered, casting a look over her shoulder. The alchemist was directly behind her and gaining, his features locked in rage. He sent another thunderbolt at her, and she pulled up hard on Starfire's neck as the echoing boom made her teeth rattle. "Get me above him," she urged.

The young Omera turned sharply and beat his wings hard, flying straight up until he was above the other pair. Then Abigail let go, dropping down onto Vertulious's back. She fisted her hands into the fabric of his robes as he tried to shrug her off.

The shreek-Omera turned its head and snapped its jaws, but it couldn't reach her. Abigail flung her weight sideways to unseat the he-witch. With nothing to hold on to, suddenly they were spiraling through the air. They hit the water with a loud splash. His heavy robes smothered her, and she flailed, trying to free herself, but his bony fingers dug into her shoulders and held her underwater. She kicked and fought as panic set in, and then a sharp fin smacked against her, knocking her free of his grasp.

Abigail spun around. Mermaids swirled in the water. They parted to reveal Queen Capricorn floating in a large bubble. The queen beckoned Abigail forward. Abigail looked up, but Vertulious had disappeared. Her lungs burned, but she swam toward the bubble, passing through it easily. It sealed behind her, and she dragged in a grateful breath.

"Take this." The queen pressed the spellbook into Abigail's hands. "You must get Vertulious to return to it. It is the only way to contain his powers. Throw it into the sea when he is trapped. We will bury it in the deepest part of the ocean, never to be found."

"I don't know if I can defeat him," Abigail said. "He's too powerful."

Capricorn reached up to her crown and removed the teardrop stone, then lifted the sea emerald that hung around Abigail's neck. She pressed the teardrop into the sea emerald. Instantly, a bright light shone out.

"Your mother's gift has great power. Use it wisely," the sea queen said, and then with a flick of her tail, the bubble burst, and she was gone.

As Abigail floated, her fingers went to her throat. The white stone sat in the center of the sea emerald, blazing with white light. Energy zinged through her veins. With a strong kick, she swam upward and broke the surface of the water. Starfire swooped down, and she grabbed his wing and hauled herself onto his back.

"Let's finish this," she said.

# Chapter 28

By the time Abigail reached the open field in front of the gates of Skara Brae, much had changed. Two of the giants had been knocked down by clever Balfins who'd tied ropes around their ankles. The rest of the Balfin army was attacking the walls of the fortress, barely held back by the Orkadian Guard. Swords clanged in the air, ringed by the shouts of the men and women fighting bravely.

Vertulious flew around Utgard-Loki, sending bolt after bolt of lightning at the giant, who staggered backward, fending off the attacks with the head of the hammer.

Abigail set Starfire down and slid off his back. She placed the spellbook on the ground and called up a ball of witchfire. The witchfire wasn't green. It wasn't blue—not even purple. It was a dazzling white, and it burned brighter than anything she had ever seen.

She cocked her arm back and threw it straight at the awful shreek-Omera she had helped create. It let out a high-pitched scream as the white fire engulfed it. Its wings collapsed, sending it tumbling to the ground. Vertulious managed to leap clear, but the shreek-Omera was finished.

Power hummed in Abigail's veins. "Surrender," she called out, "or I will destroy you."

Vertulious responded with a blast of witchfire mixed with thunder. She deflected the first attack with one of her own, but a second blast followed so fast she took a hit that sent her flying. She rolled in the dirt, but Vertulious wasn't finished. He sent another blast, advancing on her. Abigail scrambled back, but the witchfire singed her arm. Another blast burned her leg. She kept trying to get a blast off, but he was relentless.

Robert dashed in, swinging something around his head. Small stones lifted off the ground and pelted Vertulious, turning his attention away from Abigail. Robert was swinging his pouch, she realized, the one that held Odin's Stone. The stone must contain some residual magic. He swung it harder, driving Vertulious back three steps before the he-witch sent the boy hurtling through the air with a curt wave of his hand.

Still, it gave Abigail time to recover and get off her own blast. It hit Vertulious on the shoulder, making him flinch. He crossed Thor's gauntlets together, and searing lightning erupted from his fingers. The lightning forked across the field, trapping her in its embrace. Her body lifted off the ground, held in the powerful charge. Pain flared as every nerve cell ignited. Her jaw clenched as she tried to fight it, to break the field of energy around her, but she was failing.

And then something blocked the lightning. It was Hugo. He had run out onto the field with a shield and stepped into the blast. It blew him sideways, but not before he'd deflected the lightning back at Vertulious, forcing the he-witch to dive to the side.

Glorian stood over Abigail and thrust her hand out. "Get up."

"I can't do it." Abigail blinked back tears. "I can't defeat him."

"You're Abigail Tarkana. You're the Curse Breaker. Everyone knows it. So get up."

Abigail let the girl help her to her feet. Her body trembled with pain, and her knees wobbled.

"What do you need?" Glorian asked.

"Witchfire. Lots of it." Abigail took a shaky breath.

Glorian took a stand at her side, hands raised. Safina appeared at her other side, digging the toe of her boot in the dirt. "I'll help."

On Glorian's right, Nelly slunk up. "No one messes with the coven," she said, clenching her taloned fingers.

Abigail's spirits fluttered. *Maybe. Just maybe . . .*

"Together on my count," she said.

"On *my* count," a cool voice interjected. Endera stepped up, elbowing in beside her. "Don't be so bossy, Abigail."

If things hadn't been so serious, Abigail might have smiled.

Across the field, Vertulious shook with laughter. "Do you really think a pathetic band of witchlings can stop *me*? The greatest he-witch to ever live?" He stalked forward. "I will incinerate you where you stand." He put his fingers to his lips and let out a piercing whistle. The battle halted as the Balfin army lowered their weapons and the witches landed their Omeras. On the rampart walls, the Orkadians lined up, watching.

"Let this be a lesson to any who challenge me," he called. "Witness my power and surrender now before I obliterate you from existence." Vertulious cracked his neck to the side, drawing his hands together, and thrust them out. A ball of witchfire appeared in front of him, growing larger and larger until it rose above their heads. He crossed the gauntlets, and the ball filled with crackling lightning.

Endera called up a ball of witchfire. "Ready?"

"Oh, yeah," Nelly said, calling up her own.

The witchlings each called up a ball of witchfire, joining it with Endera's to form a large ball of witchfire. Abigail added hers last, the white fire mixing with the green.

"And now you will perish." The he-witch threw his hands forward.

"Now!" Endera shouted, and the witchlings threw their hands forward.

The two enormous balls of witchfire flew across the field and met in the center. His easily overtook theirs, pushing it back toward them. The heat of its core washed over them.

They kept up a steady stream of witchfire, but the ball of witchfire was inching closer and closer to them.

"More!" Abigail cried. "We need more."

Blistering heat made her break out into a sweat. Any second now and it would consume them.

Next to her, Safina began to recite loudly. "A witch's heart is made of stone. Cold as winter, I cut to the bone."

The ball of witchfire moved forward away from them a few inches.

Nelly joined in, her voice strained. "My witch's soul is black as tar, forged in darkness to leave a scar."

Their witchfire grew larger, gaining another inch toward Vertulious.

"My witch's blood, it burns with power." Sweat poured down Glorian's face. "Cross me not, or you will cower."

A surge of energy rushed through Abigail. It was working. Their witchfire was growing with every verse.

"My witch's hands will conjure evil," Endera said. "I plot and plan. I'm quite deceitful." She stomped her front

foot, straining harder as the witchfire poured from their hands into the glowing mass that stood between them.

The two balls of witchfire were equal in size now. Hope made a crazy dance along Abigail's spine as she said the final verse. "My witch's tongue will speak a curse, to bring you misery and so . . . much . . . worse."

With the final word, she closed her eyes. *Please, mother. I need your help.* The white stone at her chest sent out a blinding light into the center of their ball of witchfire, and with a sudden *whoosh*, the two balls became one, turning bright white and growing even larger as it descended on the he-witch.

Vertulious backpedaled, trying to escape it, but he couldn't outrun the ball of white fire that consumed him. His arms spread out as he was held in the center of it. They could see his body shaking and jerking about inside the glowing ball of fire.

The teardrop stone glowed brighter and brighter at Abigail's chest until, with a blinding flash, it exploded, shattering the necklace into pieces that fell at her feet.

Abigail dropped her arms. The other witchlings did the same, all panting with exertion.

The massive ball of witchfire winked out.

Vertulious swayed left, then right, then fell forward. From the pocket of his robe, a red apple rolled.

"We did it." Abigail looked at Endera. For once, the girl gave a small smile, then quickly looked away. Glorian whooped and slapped Nelly on the back.

Safina frowned. "What's *he* doing?"

Abigail turned. Robert had walked over to the unconscious Vertulious, taken the gauntlets and Belt of Strength off him, and strapped them on.

"Robert—no!"

"Release the hammer," he shouted at Utgard-Loki. The giant opened his hand, and the hammer flew to Robert.

"Now I'm going to fix things." The boy raised the weapon. "I am going to erase this parasite from this world—scatter him in so many pieces he will be nothing more than dust motes in the wind."

Vertulious raised his head, still weakened from the witchlings' attack. His hand reached for the apple, but Robert kicked the fruit aside. He stood over the he-witch, prepared to release the hammer, but Abigail stepped between them.

"No. You cannot use that against a witch."

Robert waved the hammer at her. "Step aside, Abigail, or I will throw this right through you."

"No, you won't . . . you can't."

"Why not?"

"Because it will start a new war, and then it will never end. I will deal with him, I promise. Put it down."

Robert wavered, then lowered the hammer.

Abigail turned to Vertulious. "You can't win. Surrender, and we'll find a way to make peace."

The old alchemist staggered to his feet. His hair hung over his face, and his robe was singed and torn. "They will destroy us all," he said to the witches, who stood staring. He took a lurching step forward. "We cannot surrender now."

"No. They will make peace, won't you?" Abigail pleaded as Lord Barconian rode up and dismounted from his horse. The Orkadian soldier looked torn.

"Father, peace is what we want, is it not?" Robert asked.

He put a hand on the boy's shoulder. "Yes. We will make peace if Hestera will agree."

"No! Hestera is not in charge of this coven. I am!" Vertulious shouted, calling up another ball of witchfire. He tried to fling it at Lord Barconian but a bolt of lightning struck the ground at his feet.

A golden-haired god broke through the throng of soldiers, riding on a chariot pulled by two fierce-looking goats. He skidded to a halt, jumped down, and strode over to them.

"Hand over Mjolnir now, or none will leave this field alive." Thunder rumbled, and lightning swirled over their heads.

Robert set the hammer down, then took off the gauntlets and Belt of Strength and handed them over to the god. Thor strapped them on and held his hand out. The hammer flew to his hand, and he quickly sheathed it at his side.

Thor breathed a sigh of relief before turning to glare accusingly at Abigail. "You stole my hammer and deceived me using the name of a dear friend."

"I didn't want to," Abigail said. "It was for a good reason."

"To what end? To use my hammer for war?"

"No, to stop a war!" she cried. "Please believe me. I wanted to find a way to bring balance. Vertulious had too much power—without Odin's Stone, there could never be peace."

"You are a witch, are you not?"

"Yes, but—"

"And did you not steal it that your coven might destroy these innocent people?"

"No!" Hugo and Robert said at once.

Robert stepped forward. "I am Robert Barconian, Son of Odin, and I stand for her. She wouldn't let me use it to finish off that one." He pointed at Vertulious. "She said it would only bring more war."

The god frowned at the huddled figure, his brows drawing together. "Who is that? It can't be . . ."

"That's Vertulious," Abigail said. "An ancient alchemist who was brought back to life."

"Of course, I know him." Thor stalked forward, gripped Vertulious by his robes, and hauled him close. "He stole one of my father's sacred apples. I confronted him, but he disappeared into some kind of spellbook."

"This spellbook." Abigail retrieved the spellbook from where she had placed it. "He's the reason Odin's Stone was destroyed. He discovered the formula to create an apple of the gods." Clasping the spellbook, she picked up the apple that had fallen from Vertulious's pocket and handed it to the god. "It restored him, and then he planted a tree with the seeds. He's determined to wage war with the Orkadians."

"So you thought it all right to use my hammer to settle things?" Thor rolled the apple around in his hand. "My father should have never brought these islands into this realm. I've told him that many times."

"But he did," Abigail said, "because he cared about the people. Even the witches," she added. "There were those that saw good in them."

"Well, they were wrong, weren't they?" Thor said. "Look at where you are now—all I see is the same power-hungry evil that has always been there. I don't see any good witches."

"There aren't many," she agreed. "But surely one is reason enough to hope."

# Chapter 29

The god stared silently at her. "The matter of war shall not be settled with my hammer. You must find a way for agreement among yourselves, or I will have to report to my father that his experiment of bringing magical creatures into Asgard is a failure."

"We can agree, right, Robert?" Abigail turned to him.

"That's up to your coven, isn't it?" he said.

"And your father."

Lord Barconian stepped forward. "I am always willing to discuss peaceful negotiations."

"The witches will never stop," the Eifalian named Gael said as he joined them.

"No, the witchling is right," Lord Barconian said. "Where there is one who believes in peace, there is hope. Hestera, what say you to another chance at harmony between us? Resume our lives and coexist?"

Hestera hobbled forward, leaning heavily on her cane. "War was never my idea. It was always that Vertulious."

"Madame," her lieutenant pleaded at her side. "The Balfin army is the finest in the land. We can defeat them with our sheer might."

"Silence!" Hestera snapped. "Your men failed me today. I will not forget that."

Lord Barconian extended his hand, but the witch turned away.

"I said we would coexist, not be friends."

"What of Vertulious?" Lord Barconian asked, withdrawing his hand.

"He is your problem to deal with now." Hestera snapped her fingers and disappeared, leaving a cloud of purple smoke.

The other witches mounted their Omeras and took flight. The Balfin soldiers grumbled but began making their way toward the beach and the rowboats waiting to take them back to their ships.

"What will you do with him?" Abigail let the spellbook fall open a crack in her arms. "He's still powerful—there is no prison that will hold him."

"This one is coming with me to face trial by the gods." Thor gripped the he-witch's robes. "He will spend eternity regretting his actions."

But before Thor could haul the alchemist away, Vertulious began to vaporize, disappearing in a trail of smoke into the waiting spellbook.

When he was gone, only his robe remained.

"What have you done, child?" Thor demanded.

"What needed to be done," Abigail said, snapping the book closed. "Vertulious would never have gone willingly into the spellbook. Only the threat of you taking him to Asgard would do it."

"But how will he face punishment now?" Thor asked.

"Oh, he'll be punished." She grinned. "He thinks he can control things from the spellbook, but he can't when no one's around to listen to him."

She walked to the edge of the cliffs, cocked her arm back,

and threw the book into the sea. A silver fin lashed in the air, and the book disappeared underwater.

"The mermaids will make sure it's buried under a rock deep in the sea. It will be centuries before Vertulious ever sees the light of day."

"You planned that?" Thor sounded impressed. "For a witchling, you're rather clever."

"I'm not sure I'm still a witchling." Abigail watched the departing sails of the Balfin ships. "I don't know if Madame Hestera will let me back in."

"If not, there is always a place for you with me," Thor said. "I owe a great debt of gratitude not only to your father but to you as well, for making sure my hammer wasn't used in an evil way."

"I'm sorry I tricked you," she said.

He winked at her. "Apparently I am easily tricked. You can make up for it by promising to destroy that apple tree. Such power cannot be allowed to exist outside of my father's walls."

"You have my word."

"I'll hold you to it. Now, giant"—he turned to Utgard-Loki—"I have a thing or two to say to you." He whistled for his goats to follow with his chariot.

"Not again." Utgard-Loki groaned as they walked back to the sea. "My brain is very tired."

Lord Barconian put his hand on Abigail's shoulder. "You saved many lives today."

"Thank you."

"You are always welcome here." He nodded to Abigail and Hugo and walked away toward his men.

Rego gave Abigail a quick bow. "That was some fine magic today. I hope we meet again under better circumstances."

"Me too," she said.

Mullet ruffled her hair, and Obie thwacked Hugo on the back. Then it was just Robert and Hugo.

"So I guess it's goodbye," Robert said.

Abigail smiled. "Thanks for standing up for me."

"And me," Hugo added.

"It's what friends do." He threw his arms around Abigail in an awkward hug. "I'll miss you."

"And I you."

She stepped back, and Robert slapped Hugo on the shoulder. "Need to improve your sword work if you're going to be a soldier."

"No more soldiering for me," Hugo said. "I'm going back to being a scientist."

"How will you get home?" Robert asked.

"Like this." Abigail put two fingers in her mouth and whistled.

A shadow crossed the ground as a pair of dark figures circled overhead before landing next to them.

Starfire squealed with excitement as he nuzzled Abigail, but Abigail's eyes were on Big Mama. The proud Omera held her head high, eyes blazing with triumph. With Vertulious gone, his hold over the Omeras was over.

Abigail wrapped her arms around Big Mama's scaly neck. "I'm sorry," she whispered.

The Omera snuffled loudly and moaned deep in her throat, letting out the pain she had endured.

"So you're not mad at me?" Abigail asked.

Big Mama snorted and headbutted her again.

Abigail grinned. "Good. Because we need a ride. And one for our friends." She turned to look at the three witchlings that huddled in a small circle.

"Friends?" Endera sniffed, folding her arms. "Don't push it. We can make our own way back."

"Oh, stuff it, Endera," Nelly said. "I'm not riding on a crowded ship when I can fly on the back of that beasty."

Starfire lowered his wing, and Nelly climbed on, followed by Glorian and lastly Endera.

The young Omera took a short hop and sped into the air. It wobbled once, then gained altitude. Nelly's cries of excitement could be heard as Starfire wheeled out over the sea.

Abigail put a hand on Big Mama's neck and pulled herself up. "Until the next adventure," she said to Robert.

"Count me in." He saluted her with his sword. "I'll write you letters."

She smiled. "I'd like that."

Hugo climbed up behind Abigail, and they took off, heading for the sea.

"Hold on," Hugo said. "Can you land on the beach?"

Abigail guided Big Mama down.

Hugo slipped off the Omera's back and walked across the sand. "Oskar, is that you?"

From behind a rock, a boy poked his head out. "Is it over?"

"Yes, but you have to come now, or you'll be left behind."

"I'm not riding on that . . . that . . . beast," he said, eyes wide with terror.

Abigail urged Big Mama closer. The Omera snapped her teeth, and the boy cowered back.

"Abigail, stop it," Hugo said. "She won't bite, trust me." He climbed back onto Big Mama and held his hand out. After a moment, the boy grasped it and gingerly climbed up behind him.

"Hold on," Abigail said. "You're in for a wild ride."

The Omera gathered her haunches and launched into the air. They waved goodbye to Robert as his form grew smaller and smaller until the island disappeared from view.

# Chapter 30

It was evening when they landed on the shores of Balfour Island. Endera and the others flew straight to the Tarkana Fortress. Hugo and Abigail descended onto the grass in front of the Balfin School for Boys and waved grateful goodbyes to Big Mama.

"Thanks," Oskar said, eyes downcast. "I'd appreciate it if . . . you don't . . . that is . . ."

"Tell everyone how you were a solid lookout?"

Oskar raised grateful eyes, then shook his head. "You're all right, Suppermill. I'm sorry I was such a sneevil's butt. See you at school." The boy turned and hurried off.

"That was quite something," Abigail said.

Hugo looked pleased with himself. "I think we fixed everything."

"Not everything. Baba Nana is still in a coma, and we have to find that apple tree Vertulious planted and destroy it."

"We'll find it. And a cure for Baba Nana. At least the war is over."

"Do you think there will ever be another one?"

"One thing about war, it never seems to completely end, does it?"

Abigail sighed. "Not as long as there are witches who want more power."

Hugo's expression clouded. "Would you have . . . I mean . . . the raven . . . what Safina said."

"You mean would I have betrayed you? Left you in Jotunheim to die?"

He nodded, a pained look on his face.

She wanted to be angry at him for even thinking it, but instead she put a finger to her chin. "I did think about it, but what would a giant want with someone as puny as you? No, if I wanted to get rid of you, I would have found a nasty viken to devour you, but last time you faced a viken, you sent it into a pit of quicksand, so maybe a sneevil. That's it, a pack of them. That's what I would have done."

He grinned. "You're making fun of me."

She punched him lightly on the arm. "Yes, because you already know the answer. Like it or not, if I had to choose between you and my coven—I'd choose you, Hugo."

He nodded rapidly, his eyes bright. Then he pointed at her chest. "Your sea emerald. It's gone now. How will you hide your blue witchfire?"

Abigail shrugged. "I guess it's time I was just myself— if Madame Hestera lets me back in."

Hugo looked over his shoulder in the direction of his little house. "I should be going. My parents will be worried sick, and Emenor will be wanting to pound on me for good measure. I'll see you after school?"

"I'll be there." She gave him a swift hug, holding him an extra second, before turning to walk through the woods toward the Tarkana Fortress.

Abigail entered through the small garden gate and sat under their favorite jookberry tree. She peeled her wool cap off, leaning back against the trunk. The air held only a mild chill compared to the realm of the giants. The blue star twinkled faintly in the darkening sky.

"Father, I tried hard to fix my mistakes," she said. "I hope you would be proud of me."

There was a rustle of wind, and when Abigail turned her head, Vor, the goddess of wisdom, was sitting next to her. Anger furrowed her brow.

"Abigail, what have you done?"

Abigail blinked. "I don't . . . I thought . . . I mean . . . I stopped the war. I thought you would be pleased."

The goddess gripped her arm tightly. "Did you pass the spellbook on to a sea creature named Capricorn?"

A cold lick of fear ran up Abigail's spine. "Yes. She helped me trap Vertulious. She promised to bury his magic deep in the sea."

The goddess looked pained, shaking her head. "No, Abigail. She deceived you. She is a wicked, evil creature. She used the magic in the spellbook to unlock the prison of a very, very dangerous creature."

"Who?"

"Jormungand."

"Jormungand? You mean the Midgard Serpent?"

"Yes. The one who would swallow the world if allowed."

"Why would Capricorn do that?"

"My visions do not show me everything, but, Abigail, the serpent must be returned to its prison under the sea, or it won't be just Orkney that is wiped out of existence but the entire universe."

# Epilogue

Hestera made her way into her chambers, feeling every ache in every joint. The day had been a fiasco. They had been humiliated once again. The only saving grace was that that power-hungry fool Vertulious was gone, and the coven was completely hers again.

She opened the door to her chamber and went inside, snapping her fingers to light the fire. As flames licked up in the hearth, she was taken aback by the sight of a figure seated in front of the fire.

"Who's there?" she demanded.

The figure sat forward, and Hestera nearly shrieked with terror.

"Hello, old friend."

"Capricorn. What do you want?" Hestera eased down into the chair opposite the creature.

Queen Capricorn fluttered a hand in the air. "I hear your war did not end well. A shame. I would have liked to see those helpless Orkadians on their knees."

"There will be another time," Hestera grated out.

"So you say. Every time."

"I am tired. If you came to mock me, come another day."

The mermaid rose. "I came to give a message. Your war may have failed, but mine will bring down the walls of Asgard."

"Yours?" Hestera's stony heart skipped a beat. "What do you mean?"

"Didn't you hear? I released my favorite pet from his cage."

An icy fear filled Hestera's veins. "No. You wouldn't." Surely she wasn't that crazy . . .

"I would. You remember Jormungand? He has a bone to pick with the gods of Asgard. I know I can count on your help if I need it, can I not, old friend?"

Hestera gripped the knob of her cane, weighing her options, and then she slowly nodded. "Whatever you might need."

# THE END

# About the Author

Alane Adams is an author, professor, and literacy advocate. She is the author of the Legends of Orkney, Witches of Orkney, and Legends of Olympus fantasy mythology series for tweens and *The Coal Thief*, *The Egg Thief*, and *The Santa Thief* picture books for early-grade readers. She lives in Southern California.

*Author photo © Melissa Coulier/Bring Media*

# SELECTED TITLES FROM SPARKPRESS

SparkPress is an independent boutique publisher delivering high-quality, entertaining, and engaging content that enhances readers' lives, with a special focus on female-driven work. www.gosparkpress.com

*Caley Cross and the Hadeon Drop*, J. S. Rosen, $16.95, 978-1-68463-053-0. When thirteen-year-old Caley Cross, an orphan with a dark power, is guided by a jumpsuit-wearing mole into another world—Erinath—she finds a place deeply rooted in nature where the people have animal-like powers and she is a Crown Princess—but she soon learns that the most powerful evil being in *any* world is waiting for her there.

*The Blue Witch: The Witches of Orkney, Book One*, Alane Adams. $12.95, 978-1-943006-77-9. Nine-year-old Abigail Tarkana has a problem: her witch magic has finally come in, but it's *different*—and being different is a problem at the Tarkana Witch Academy. Together with her scientist-friend Hugo, she face off against sneevils, shreeks, and vikens in a race to discover the secrets about her mysterious magic.

*The Rubicus Prophecy: Witches of Orkney, Book 2*, Alane Adams. $12.95, 978-1-943006-98-4. As Abigail enters her second year at the Tarkana Witch Academy, she is up to her ears studying for Horrid Hexes and Awful Alchemy. But when an Orkadian warship arrives carrying troubling news, Abigail and Hugo are swept into a puzzling mystery when they help a new friend go after a missing item—one that might spell the end of everything they know.

*Red Sun: The Legends of Orkney, Book 1*, Alane Adams. $17, 978-1-940716-24-4. After learning that his mom is a witch and his missing father is a true Son of Odin, 12-year-old Sam Baron must travel through a stonefire to the magical realm of Orkney on a quest to find his missing friends and stop an ancient curse.

*Eye of Zeus: Legends of Olympus Book 1*, Alane Adams. $12.95, 978-1-68463-028-8. Finding out she's the daughter of Zeus is not what a foster kid like Phoebe Katz expected to hear from a talking statue of Athena. But when her beloved social worker is kidnapped, Phoebe and her two friends must travel back to ancient Greece and rescue him before she accidentally destroys Olympus.

# About SparkPress

S parkPress is an independent, hybrid imprint focused on merging the best of the traditional publishing model with new and innovative strategies. We deliver high-quality, entertaining, and engaging content that enhances readers' lives. We are proud to bring to market a list of *New York Times* best-selling, award-winning, and debut authors who represent a wide array of genres, as well as our established, industry-wide reputation for creative, results-driven success in working with authors. SparkPress, a BookSparks imprint, is a division of SparkPoint Studio LLC.

Learn more at GoSparkPress.com